ONE, WIZARD PLACE

BY

D.M. PAUL

ILLUSTRATIONS BY FRANK BERGER

This book is dedicated to my wife and daughter, for their love and support.

I'd like to send special thanks to Deanna Brady for her excellence in editing. She can be found at getwords@aol.com. I would also like to thank Leslie Cholowsky for bringing this project together and preparing this book for electronic-publishing. She can be found at www.booksunbound.com. Without them this book would still be supporting the short leg of my kitchen table.

Book 1 – One Wizard Place
Book 2 – Sentinel
Book 3 – Sidhe

Visit

www.onewizardplace.com

CONTENTS

ONE
Nixies

TWO
Cloudview

THREE
The Incantation Enforcement Agency

FOUR
The Great Forest

FIVE
The Swamp of Doom and Despair

SIX
The Ocean of Sand

SEVEN
Moog

EIGHT
Blood Dragon

-Chapter One-
Nixies

s. Willeby's house was usually as neat and trim as a house could be. On any given day in the past, her quaint little cottage could easily have made the cover of a magazine… but lately she has been lucky to stay off the six o'clock news.

It *was* quite a mess. What was left of her white picket fence was scattered and broken into a pile of

1

twigs and bent nails. Her big, blue-ribbon rose bushes, with their enormous red petals, lay trampled across her formerly green lawn. Like a scene in an old war movie, potholes littered the once perfectly manicured front yard. Just about all the windows were shattered, with all sorts of household belongings hanging and dangling from the broken frames. An old cowboy boot had even managed to get itself stuffed into her mailbox.

Yes, old Ms. Willeby definitely had herself a nixie problem, and a fairly big one at that.

With his faithful partner by his side, agent Justin Kasey Hobskin--generally known as "Kase"--strolled through the front yard of their latest assignment. Kase's partner, Murdox, sniffed at the remains of the lawn as they went along.

Murdox, formerly a grouchy, irritable, and generally bad-tempered wizard, had been cursed with the body of a wolf-dog when he and his previous partner were attacked by an evil witch doctor.

"I hope this gig includes some decent food, at least," Murdox remarked, snuffling an empty candy wrapper. "All I had for lunch was a lousy sliced-cheese sandwich."

Shaking his head, Kase concluded that Murdox had nothing useful to say, as usual.

Murdox sensed Kase's reaction and peered up at him in the piercing way that only a dog can. "I'm a wolf-dog now, remember? Dogs mostly eat, sleep, and p...."

"Enough! I get the point."

For almost as long as Kase could remember, Murdox had been notoriously ornery--but since his wizardly powers and human form had been taken from him, he had been even crankier than ever.

The two of them slowed as they approached the steps leading to the front door of Ms. Willeby's house. Kase tightened the straps of his backpack, tucked his shirttail into his pants, and ran his fingers through his hair. He glanced down at Murdox and frowned in dismay. Then he ran his hand over the wolf-dog's coat, slicked down some flyaway fur, and attempted to smooth his ears. This accomplished nothing but to elicit a low, guttural growl from Murdox, to which Kase paid no attention.

They slowly climbed the four steps to the house,

and Kase rang the doorbell. There was a crash, a thud, and quite a few thumps. After a bit, a frail voice responded, "Yes. Who's there?"

"Ms. Willeby?" Kase replied, "It's Kase and Murdox from the Incantation Enforcement Agency, Counter-Curse Division. We got your message and came over as quickly as we could. We're here to help!"

The bright red door eased open about halfway and then suddenly fell off its hinges. It landed with a thud on the front porch. Luckily Kase and Murdox were able to scramble out of the way before it could squash them.

"Dear me, I'm so terribly sorry!" said Ms. Willeby. "Those troublesome little monsters must have pulled the pins right out of the hinges."

Kase and Murdox quickly regained their composure and stepped over the fallen door. Kase glanced quickly around the house, and Murdox stuck his snout in the air and took a couple of sniffs. They muttered to themselves disapprovingly, but it was Kase who spoke first.

"Not to worry, Ma'am. We've had to deal with

nixies before. A terrible lot they are! Tell me, Ms. Willeby, how did you get mixed up with them?"

Suddenly a stink bomb exploded in the middle of the living room with a *boom!* and a ghastly green cloud billowed toward them. Ms. Willeby moved very rapidly for her age. Covering her nose, she followed close behind Kase and Murdox as they dove off the stairs onto the ruined lawn.

Ms. Willeby waved her hand toward her little front yard and began to whimper. "It's all my fault! All I wanted to do was conjure up some garden gnomes to help me tidy my roses."

Murdox and Kase stood by patiently as she spoke. They were not as interested in what she was saying as they were in allowing time for the air to clear.

"The annual Wizards' Day parade is coming up, you know, and I wanted my little garden to look its best." She sighed deeply and then continued. "I gathered up all the proper ingredients for gnome casserole. I prepared the spell and baked it in the oven at four-hundred-fifty degrees, just like the recipe calls for. But Ms. Tilly... you know old Ms. Tilly, don't you? She stopped by to share a cup of tea and some really juicy tidbits of news about the Reverend Heartgood. Well, we lost all track of time, and I guess I cooked the little fellows too long."

Kase nodded to her supportively as he dragged off his brown leather backpack with the IEA logo displayed on its front pouch. He unzipped the bag and reached inside. After a short search, he pulled out a large leather-bound book entitled *The Joy of Conjuring, Third Edition*. He quickly shuffled through the pages to the chapter called "Gnome Incantations Made Easy."

Kase skimmed through the spell and then shook his head as he reached the Helpful Hints section. After a brief consultation with Murdox, he turned to the section on nixies and scanned the incantation. Kase then asked Ms. Willeby where she had purchased the ingredients-- particularly the imp brains.

Ms. Willeby turned an unflattering shade of red and looked around sheepishly. "Well, the Wizard's Market was all sold out of fresh imp brains, so I went to the regular grocer's and picked up the canned variety."

Kase glanced at Murdox, who curled his lip. "Do

you happen to remember which brand you purchased, Ms. Willeby?"

Ms. Willeby stared at Kase with a worried look in her eyes, trying to recall. "I believe I chose Blue Ogre brains…. Yes, I'm sure of it. It was definitely the Blue Ogre brand."

"Well, that explains it. My reference book cautions against using certain varieties of canned brains because some manufacturers pickle them for longer shelf-life. Blue Ogre just happens to be at the top of the list."

Ms. Willeby paled until she looked downright ghostly. "I must have conjured up those little guys a hundred times before. I hardly look at the recipe anymore. Dear, dear me... I never even realized…!"

"Not to worry, Ms. Willeby. We see these kinds of errors happen all the time." Kase cleared his throat and nudged Murdox, who was rolling his eyes and snorting.

Kase gave Murdox a stern glance. "Unfortunately, overcooked pickled imp brains are a perfect recipe for disaster, and in this case they transformed your gnomes into nixies."

The young agent dropped *The Joy of Conjuring, Third Edition* back into his backpack. "Not to worry!" he assured her. "We've come prepared."

Kase dug around in his backpack again. After pulling out and setting aside a billfold, a set of car keys, a television remote control, and a pair of old socks, he continued searching until he finally came up with a gigantic mayonnaise jar.

This was no ordinary mayonnaise jar. Instead of being filled with mayonnaise, it was packed full of small forms suspended in a glowing gelatin-like goo. It almost looked like something you might eat in a school cafeteria… except that these weren't suspended fruit pieces. These chunks were very irate little blue creatures.

Setting the mayonnaise jar to the side, Kase reached back into his pack again and pulled out and then replaced several odd-looking contraptions in succession and muttered to himself for awhile. Finally, he located a small ream of flypaper wrapped tightly in yellow plastic. He looked up to see Mrs. Willeby staring at the mayonnaise jar.

"I have no idea how it works, myself," Kase told her. "The instruction book says something about a quantum compressor shifting the multidimensional time/space continuum. All I know is that you can keep stuffing the little creeps into the jar, and they'll just shrink to fit."

With a smile and a flourish, Kase held up the jar so she could get a better look. The label read: *Jellied Nixies.*

"This is where we are going to put your problem, Ms. Willeby."

Ms. Willeby looked very impressed.

Murdox just looked as if he were going to spit up a hair ball… if dogs could have hair balls.

"This is how it's going to play out."

Kase proceeded to explain to the others what seemed to be a hastily improvised but workable plan.

Kase and Murdox then left Ms. Willeby safe in the front yard while they gathered up their supplies and tiptoed back into the devastated house. Kase carefully unwrapped the yellow plastic around the ream of flypaper. He peeled one sheet of very sticky paper from the roll and looked for a good place to set his trap. He spotted the coffee table, still covered with the splattered remains of Ms. Willeby's and Ms. Tilly's afternoon tea.

Kase dragged the coffee table to the middle of the living room and placed the flypaper on top of it. With great care, Murdox dropped Kase's keys on top of the sticky paper. Then the investigators slipped behind the couch and waited for their quarry.

They didn't have to wait very long.

They heard a thunderous howl, followed by some seriously foul language.

Kase started to get up from behind the couch, but Murdox quickly grabbed his shirttail and pulled him back down. "Take it easy, Trigger. Remember that nixies are stupid… and by that I mean really, really stupid. If we wait just a bit longer…."

*"$#@%, $@%#, *&*$%** !!!!!"*

Another nixie had been captured in the flypaper and was blurting out a series of words that would get a kid grounded for life.

Murdox sniffed the air. "Okay, now we can

check it out."

When they poked their heads up over the couch, they saw two little blue-skinned creatures fighting over the set of car keys as they tangled themselves in the sticky paper. Kase looked at Murdox and gestured with his lips in an expression that said *Hey, I'm impressed!*

Murdox grunted. "Yes, the plan is working. I've done this before, too, you know. I may be a wolf-dog now, but keep in mind that I was a wizard before this."

Kase studied the pointy ears, the furry tail, and the drooling tongue. It was often hard to remember that Murdox had once had another form.

As Murdox had read to him on their way there, *The Great Big Anthology of Annoying Creatures* defined *nixies* as "creatures between 1½ and 2 feet tall, having large, pointed ears, big yellow eyes, and ropy, mottled hair that grows in every conceivable color and direction." It continued, "Most commonly, their skin appears as various shades of blue, but it may range to a deep purple. Nixies are usually seen dressed in shabby bits of rags or other trappings they have swiped from whomever they are currently tormenting. They are dimwitted creatures with an insatiable appetite for thieving and causing mayhem. Nixies are notorious for being at the center of trouble. Though it has never been proven, it's generally believed that they were the cause of the Green-out of '29, a tumultuous period in history when everything turned a pale shade of puce."

Fortunately for Kase and Murdox, nixies had a reputation for being as dumb as tree stumps. According to the book, "Their overwhelming desire to pilfer allows them to be lured easily into a trap and captured."

Kase watched in horror as the two nasty little creatures kicked and screamed at each other while trying to free themselves from the sticky paper. It looked like a devilish game of Twister.

Kase approached the nixies carefully, avoiding their flailing arms and snapping jaws. He grabbed them both by the hair. The nixies responded with objections that brought new meaning to the phrase *bad language*. With Murdox following close behind, Kase walked out the front door holding the two furious creatures--still precariously stuck to the flypaper--at arm's length. They made their way to Ms. Willeby, who was trying to tidy her front yard.

"We caught two of them," Kase reported, "...and I'd say they're a little upset." He had trouble holding them as the two little captives shrieked and increased their wild struggle to escape. "Right! We had best put these little buggers away."

Murdox went for the large mayonnaise jar and rolled it over to Kase. Ms. Willeby unscrewed the lid and placed the jar upright on the ground.

"Hurry!" Murdox warned. "We have to stuff these vermin into the jar before any others climb out."

Just as he said this, a little blue head almost popped out of the jar. Kase quickly grabbed both of the newly captured nixies by their ankles and jammed them headfirst into the jar, right on top of the one who was trying to peer over the edge. Kase pushed down until all they could see were four little feet sinking into the iridescent goo.

Murdox quickly grabbed the lid in his teeth and passed it to Kase.

Kase swiftly screwed the lid on the jar, then glanced back at the house. "Ms. Willeby, how many of these things were loose in there?"

Ms. Willeby took a moment to think and then held up one hand with all her fingers extended. "Five."

"Well, with these two captured, that means we have three more to go. We'd better get to it."

Kase and Murdox climbed cautiously up the front steps and tiptoed back into the house. Once they were inside, Murdox looked down the hallway.

"Let's try the kitchen."

With Murdox padding silently behind him, Kase passed through the dining room. Ms. Willeby's entire china cabinet had been rifled through, and most of its contents had been smashed and dispersed in pieces across the carpet.

They entered the kitchen and saw utter devastation, ground zero of an incantation gone awry. The refrigerator had been blasted open, its contents spilled, squished, and splattered across the tile floor. All the cupboard doors had been thrown open as well. The counter tops were covered in a smorgasbord of trash that littered every nook and cranny.

Murdox nosed through the garbage and

somehow found himself a bag of cookies. He started gobbling them down before Kase could smack him on the rump.

"Sorry… sometimes it's just too hard to resist," Murdox mumbled apologetically, his mouth full of cookie.

Kase tried his best to clear away some of the trash in the middle of the kitchen. He pulled another piece of flypaper from the ream and peeled off the yellow backing. Carefully, he set it on the floor. Then he pulled out the television remote control and placed it in the middle of the sticky paper. "Nixies just can't resist these things!"

When he didn't get a sarcastic response from Murdox, Kase turned to see what was going on. "Hey, don't you think you've had enough of those?"

"I'll <chomp> be <crunch> right <gulp> there."

Kase grabbed him by the collar, and with all his might, yanked him from the room in a wake of cookie crumbs.

They found a quiet place to hide and before too long, heard a tirade of screams and shouts pouring from the kitchen. This time Kase wasn't so anxious, and they waited just a little longer. Sure enough, another set of yelps and curses joined the chorus.

The two heroes stuck their heads into the kitchen and spotted two more nixies fighting with each other and tangling themselves in the flypaper. One of the two creatures, a particularly big one, yanked the remote control out of the hands of the other nixie and clocked him over the head with it. The littlest nixie sort of wobbled back and forth a bit before falling over with a thud. The bigger nixie seemed to get a huge kick out of this and began laughing hysterically.

Kase and Murdox took this as a good opportunity and dashed into the kitchen. However, neither of them remembered that the kitchen floor was slippery and covered in trash. They both skidded across the tile and fell face-first in front of the laughing nixie.

The little monster didn't skip a beat and whacked Kase on the head with the remote control. Murdox tried to intervene, but even stuck to the flypaper, the nixie was far too quick for him. With a lunge that would make a great white shark proud, the nixie threw himself at

Murdox and bit him right on the snout.

Murdox let out a howl and shook his furry head violently. He managed to rip the nixie from the sticky paper and toss him across the room into the kitchen cabinets.

Kase jumped to his feet, slipped on an overripe tomato, and fell back on his rump. Eventually he managed to stand up and stumble his way to the cabinets where Murdox had flung the larger nixie. He grabbed the dizzy blue vermin by his ropy hair and very carefully began crossing the slippery kitchen floor.

After moaning and complaining about his bitten nose, Murdox picked up the unconscious smaller nixie, still stuck to the flypaper, and made his way quickly to the front yard.

Holding the squirming larger nixie, Kase followed Murdox outside. They found Ms. Willeby still trying unsuccessfully to tidy her yard.

"We caught two more, Ms. Willeby."

Ms. Willeby looked up at the two investigators and saw that they were covered in garbage. Both were bleeding a bit from the bites. She immediately ran over to the magic jar and unscrewed the cap. She watched Kase and Murdox unceremoniously shove their captives deep into its confines and quickly screw the lid back on. Then she took her apron from around her waist and dabbed at Murdox's nose.

Kase brushed off both Murdox and himself as best he could. Kneeling down, he reached into his backpack and pulled out a big first-aid kit. From this he withdrew some alcohol swabs and a few bandages, which he handed to Ms. Willeby. He watched as she tore open one of the swabs and carefully dabbed Murdox's nose.

Murdox immediately began yelping, *"Ouweee, ouweee, ouweee!"*

"Oh, shut up, you big baby," snapped Kase. "She's just trying to help."

Ms. Willeby unwrapped one of the bandages and stuck it on Murdox's snout. She admired her own medical handiwork briefly and patted the big wolf-dog gently on the head. Then she doctored Kase's wound.

When she was done, Kase stood up and turned toward the house. "Right! We still have one nixie to go, and the last one is typically the hardest one to catch. Let's get going, Murdox."

"Just be careful, boys. I don't want anyone getting hurt."

Anticipating the type of sarcastic retort Murdox might normally make, Kase grabbed his snout and held it shut. The two investigators then entered the house again and stopped in the dining room.

Kase pulled another piece of the flypaper from the roll and removed the yellow backing. "Let's try the billfold this time. Maybe we'll be lucky, and this one will be as stupid as his friends." He laid the flypaper gently on the dining room table. Finally, he put the billfold down in the middle of his sticky trap.

The two investigators quietly ducked behind the couch. They waited… and waited. After about twenty minutes, they decided to take a look.

First they saw a long piece of string dangling from the chandelier, which hung all the way down to the sticky flypaper. Apparently, the nixie had tied some twine to the light fixture and had lowered himself *Mission Impossible*-style to the billfold, which was now open and free of its contents.

Murdox glanced up at Kase with a pained look and let out a long sigh. "This one's not nearly as dumb."

"I'd say you're right. We're going to have to outsmart this one." Kase took a moment to think and then blurted out, "I've got an idea. Follow me."

They both went outside to find Ms. Willeby so that Kase could explain his plan to both her and Murdox.

After Kase explained the plan, he and Ms. Willeby went into the house and gathered up all the dirty laundry they could find. They each carried their piles of clothing to the laundry room and dumped them in a heap on the floor. Then he winked at Ms. Willeby and raised his voice to a level that was quite a bit louder than necessary.

"You might as well get some laundry done. …Getting rid of this last nixie might take a while… he's a smart one!"

They both loaded some of the clothing into the washing machine.

Ms. Willeby shouted back, "Oops! We can't

forget to wash all my socks."

Kase looked around the cluttered room. "No, we certainly can't," he replied, making sure his voice would carry throughout the house. "You can never have too many pairs of clean socks. Maybe we should go try to find some more."

They both walked casually out of the laundry room and sat down in front of what was left of the television.

It didn't take a minute before they heard a *thumpadee-thumpadee-thump* from the laundry room. The sounds were followed by an eruption of ear-piercing screams. Kase and Ms Willeby quickly made their way through the kitchen and into the laundry room. There, they saw Murdox sitting on top of the washing machine, happily panting with his long, doggy tongue hanging out.

Kase, Murdox, and Ms. Willeby had all known that a nixie would not be able to resist the urge to steal socks from the washing machine. Murdox had hidden beneath the pile of dirty clothes, waiting to pounce on his prey. When the time was right, it had been all too easy for him to bound from beneath the pile of clothes and slam the lid shut on the little pest inside.

Kase didn't like to see him gloat, and it had been a bit cruel of Murdox to turn on the washer, but the sound of the little vermin banging around inside the machine just seemed to make the big wolf-dog happy.

After coaxing Murdox down with a bag of cookies, Kase turned off the washer and pulled out the waterlogged nixie, which was still clutching one of the dirty socks. Kase then dragged the soggy creature into the front yard and stuffed him into the jar of jellied nixies. Then he tightened down the lid and stowed the jar safely in his backpack.

Ms. Willeby couldn't have been happier. She patted Murdox on the head and scratched him behind the ears to the point that he began kicking one of his back legs, a reaction that seemed to embarrass him greatly. Then she fed him all the chocolate chip cookies he could eat. She finally turned her attention to Kase and gave him a big hug.

While still locked in Ms. Willeby's kind embrace, Kase looked at his watch. "Well, it's getting late," he told her. "We'd better be going."

"Thank you so very much!" Ms. Willeby gushed over and over again. "If there is anything I can ever do for you, just say the word. I know! I'll bake some cookies and send them to you."

"That won't be necessary," Kase replied.

As soon as he said this, Murdox bumped him in the leg, and Kase got the point. "Okay, okay... I guess that would be very nice, Ms. Willeby."

"Good! I'll make shortbread... no, chocolate chip. Well, why not? I'll make them both!" She took a long look around and sighed. "I guess I had better clean up a bit first." With that, she made her way back into her little cottage, muttering to herself about cookies and cleaning fluid.

Kase just hoped she wouldn't get them confused. He looked at his watch again. "We might just make the five o'clock slug if we hurry."

With that, the two investigators eased out the front gate and trotted down the sidewalk in the direction of the slug stop.

-Chapter Two-
Cloudview

Kase and Murdox quickly left Ms. Willeby's street behind as the sun crept down toward the horizon. After hurrying for quite a while, Kase stopped and looked up. "The sky is a particularly nice shade of blue today."

With his snout in the air, Murdox scanned the

horizon from one end to the other. "Yeah, it certainly took long enough, but I guess the city finally got all the air-scrubbers on line. It looks like they seem to be doing a pretty good job of getting the leftover green gunk out of the sky."

It had taken years to get the sky back to a nice shade of blue after the Green-Out of '29. This was accomplished with a revolutionary invention that sucked the bad green air in, passed it through an electro-magic filter, and pumped out nice, clean, blue air. In fact, the time it took from the invention of the air-scrubbing machines to their implementation around the city was remarkably short. Unfortunately, the machines seemed to be scrubbing the air clean only around the cities. This left a greenish hue that sort of clung to the fringes of the world. In time, this too would be washed clean, but the general populace preferred to find something to complain about rather than to brag about the positive points of the city's latest clean-air project.

Kase and Murdox now strolled, casually down the sidewalk, chatting with each other about nothing in particular. Kase craned his neck, trying to get a look at all the sights.

They were walking through what appeared to be a normal neighborhood, except that there was nothing normal about the quaint little houses that lined both sides of this street. Suddenly, one of the houses began to uproot itself from its manicured lawn. Then another did the same… and another. Soon all of the houses were taking wing, as far away as he could see. They began spinning and twirling in midair, leaping over one another and barely avoiding collision. A wild dance was happening right before Kase's eyes. Then as abruptly as it had all begun, it ended. The houses drifted back to the ground, and everything appeared normal, as if nothing untoward had happened.

Unsure of what he had just seen, Kase looked at Murdox. The wolf-dog appeared entirely uninterested in the aerial display. Kase was just about to ask what that was all about when Murdox spoke. "This is our stop. Hope we didn't miss our ride."

Kase realized that Murdox had no intention of letting on anything he knew about the houses, at least for a while. He also assumed that this wasn't because the wolf-dog was holding out on him. Murdox was probably curious himself. He might just be waiting to see what would happen next... or was just making Kase wait for the heck of it.

At the intersection of Grimlock and Black Stone Lane, they reached a small flight of stone steps. Kase looked at his watch. "The slug should be along any minute. We shouldn't have to wait too long."

They climbed the steps and stood on a large, covered platform. A couple of benches had been placed there strategically for the comfort of slug patrons.

Kase slung the backpack off his shoulder and dropped it onto one of the benches. He pulled out a laminated fold-out that had *Slug Schedule* printed at the top in bold red letters. "If we catch the next ride, we should be able to pick up the V train and make it back to the office before moonrise."

Murdox simply nodded in response.

A few minutes later, a cartoon-like face materialized seemingly out of nowhere on a clock hanging on the back wall. The clock--well, actually the face--screamed, "Get up! Get up!! The slug is on the way!" Then just as quickly as it had appeared, the face morphed back into a normal clock again.

Moments later, a massive yellow-and-black-striped slug slowly oozed its way toward the platform. Strapped to its back were two long rows of bench seats filled with at least twenty passengers. The slug stopped at the station and waited for a few passengers to get off its back.

Kase dropped a couple of copper coins into the money till, and he and Murdox took seats near the tail. When everyone was seated safely, the slug pulled slowly away from the platform and headed toward its next stop.

While they were riding, Kase thought about how the slug transit got started. A few years earlier, a disgruntled wizard who had repeatedly arrived late for his job had gotten frustrated with how slowly the public transportation system moved. In a fit of rage, he'd cast a spell that transformed all the city buses into slugs. For some reason, the city council hadn't objected to this change, and the buses had remained in their bulbous new state ever since. In fact, no one complained. The slugs actually moved along a good deal faster than the former buses ever had.

Kase thought the slugs were great fun and enjoyed riding the lumbering creatures. Murdox simply thought they smelled bad.

Kase watched the neighborhoods slowly slipping by and marveled at the magically enhanced homes that were once again dancing in the air. Round and round they went, bobbing and twisting. But this time a strange looking two-story model with a red shingled roof slipped away from the dance and floated silently over the slug's head. The owner, who was working in his yard, finally realized what had happened. He began chasing after the house, yelling and shaking his fists. *"Come back here!"* he howled. *"Get back here right now!"*

Murdox noticed the perplexed look in Kase's eyes and finally took pity on him. The wolf-dog confessed that he had recently read about a few builders who had been developing the new type of housing plan. Originally the houses were supposed to dance only in their own yards, but that didn't seem to be enough for the magical buildings. When they got the urge, they simply floated away and took up residence somewhere else. Only bill collectors and junk mail managed to track them down again.

"Unfortunately," Murdox continued, "due to poor planning--and the fact that the houses seemed to have minds of their own--no one can keep them under control...."

Kase found all this a bit weird. He shook his head, sat back in his seat, and thought about how he had managed to end up in this strange world.

Kase's father, Brent Hobskin, had been a New York City police detective, and a good one at that. Kase was very young at the time, but he could still recall the painful memories. His mother had been killed in an automobile accident. His father was so devastated by this tragic event that he had trouble focusing on his work. One day, on the good advice of his supervisor, he decided he needed a long vacation.

Brent contacted his sister, Zelda, who had recently been widowed herself. She had inherited an enormous estate in the country and told Brent that she would enjoy having visitors to keep her company. The Hobskins had packed their suitcases and traveled to Aunt Zelda's house for some much-needed rest and recreation. They wanted to get as far away from the bad memories as they could. Kase recalled fondly that Aunt Zelda was the kindest and sweetest person he had ever met. Without a second thought, she had welcomed them into her home for as long as they wished to stay.

The three of them had a wonderful time in the country. Brent was forgetting his problems, and Kase was adjusting nicely to his new surroundings. Gradually, though, the father and son began to realize that Aunt Zelda was a bit odd.

In her defense, Brent liked to point out that Zelda was a very wealthy woman. With an air of mock dignity, he would say, "With wealth comes status. She can no longer be considered quirky or strange. Rather, she should be referred to as *eccentric*." Then he would chuckle to himself.

More often than not, they found her to be quite a mystery and sometimes very secretive. One of her many strange hobbies was collecting all sorts of ancient mystical memorabilia, which made her home a cluttered mess. Brent and Kase soon learned that her true passion was the study of magic… and she was more than willing to teach them what she knew. They would humor her by showing interest in her avocation and secretly have a good laugh about it when they were alone.

One day, when Brent and Kase had been feeling particularly blue, Aunt Zelda handed them an old leather backpack with a strange symbol sewn into its cover. She asked them to take it up to the attic and store it in a wooden chest she kept there. She said they would know it when they saw it.

In the attic, they located the chest easily enough. When they opened it, however, they found that it wasn't full of old moth-eaten sweaters. Instead they were surprised to discover a circular staircase that disappeared downward into the darkness. Brent and Kase couldn't believe their eyes. They were so shocked by their discovery that they could think of nothing to do but simply slam the chest shut.

Brent grabbed hold of one of the handles

attached to the side of the chest and dragged it to another spot in the attic. They opened it again, but to their surprise, there was no longer a mysterious staircase hidden under the chest. Brent slammed the chest shut and stared at the lid. Then with great hesitation, he opened the chest again to have another look. Sure enough, the same set of stairs led downward into the darkness below them.

Brent looked at his son and shrugged his shoulders. "Why don't we check it out?"

The two of them climbed into the chest and carefully descended the steps to investigate where they led. After several long minutes, they finally reached the bottom of the stairs. In front of them stood a wooden door with a shiny brass doorknob.

Brent looked over to his son, his eyebrows raised in an unspoken question. Kase appeared mystified and simply shrugged in response. Before either of them could think about it too long, Brent reached out his hand, turned the knob, and opened the door....

Brent and Kase stepped through the doorway right into the main lobby of an office building belonging to the Incantation Enforcement Agency.

A large orange orangutan wearing a floppy yellow hat with a daisy sticking out of its brim was sitting behind a circular, wood-panelled desk. She lounged quite comfortably in her chair as a telephone rang almost off the hook in front of her. Apparently, she was far more interested in polishing her fingernails than answering the incoming call.

Two heavily armed black bears wearing riot gear were cautiously escorting a handcuffed ogre through a reinforced metal door on the far side of the room. At that moment, the ogre decided he was going to try to escape. He shoved his shoulder into the armored chest of one of the bears and made a fast break for an enormous glass door. Before anyone in the room could react, two more guards burst in and tackled the ogre.

To Kase and Brent's surprise, one of the new guards appeared to be human, but the other looked like a giant weasel wearing a cheap suit. With the help of the bears, the human guard pinned the ogre to the ground. The weasel stood over them both, pointing a vicious-looking pistol at the culprit.

During the commotion, Kase squeezed past his father. The orangutan lifted her head lazily from her work, not bothered in the least by the commotion all around her, and looked at the new visitors with interest.

"Brent Hobskin, I presume?" she mused. "It's about time you showed up for work."

Brent took one look at Kase, and they both jumped back toward the door. Somehow it didn't surprise either of them to find that the stairs had disappeared. Instead, they were standing in a simple broom closet--a small, dusty room with mops and brooms leaning against the far wall--where the staircase should have been.

The best Brent could figure was that Aunt Zelda had discovered a hidden gateway to this strange world. She knew her brother and his son well enough to realize that their curiosity would get the best of them, and they would investigate the stairway. Apparently Aunt Zelda had decided that it was about time her brother found a new job, and she had arranged for him to get a position at the Incantation Enforcement Agency. Brent smiled at his sister's logic. She had probably assumed that a New

York City police detective would make a terrific agent at the IEA… even if it was in a parallel dimension.

Seeing as they could not find a way home, one thing led to another, and Brent soon accepted a full-time position with the IEA. Ultimately he was promoted to detective and partnered with Murdox, who quickly became his mentor and best friend.

Since they had arrived, Brent and his son never had never been able to locate the stairway back to their dimension. Brent had soon set about to make a life in this strange place, and they'd made the best of it.

With all the new and amazing wonders of this stairway's strange world, Kase had found himself getting into all sorts of trouble. Most of the time, it had been nothing more than a misunderstanding because of the cultural differences between his old life and this new one. Some of his problems had simply been caused by a normal boy's curiosity--and his new home had more than its share of curiosities.

The last straw for Brent had been when Kase blew up their kitchen while trying to use what he thought was a toaster. Brent decided it would be safer for Kase to come to the office with him. In a world of talking dogs and other bizarre creatures, no one found a little human boy to be of any special interest. Actually, Kase turned out to be more dependable than most of the IEA's employees, so with Murdox's help, his father had finagled an apprenticeship with the agency for Kase. The rest, as they say, was history.

Murdox jarred Kase back to the present. "Take a look at that kid on her slime board."

A small girl with long, blond pigtails was running like mad toward the rear end of the slug. With both hands she held a smooth, short, flat board that had a rounded nose and upwardly curved tail. When she got as close to the creature as she dared, the little girl tossed the board in front of her and jumped onto it. The board hit the slimy goo that trailed behind the slug and then skimmed across its glassy surface.

The girl squatted down on the board and dragged one of her hands in the slime. This caused her and the board to spin round and round. Her long blond pigtails were flapping wildly around her head like the blades on a helicopter. Then the girl pulled her hand out of the ooze and cautiously stood up. She bent her legs slightly at the knees, leaned to one side, and turned the board in the direction of the curb.

Just as she neared the edge of the curb, she stomped down on the back of the board with her trailing foot and lifted her other leg. That caused the front of the board to shoot out of the slimy goo. As the tail end of the board lifted off the surface, the girl grabbed the side of the board and pulled it out from under her feet.

Kase and Murdox got a good view of the bottom of the board, which read Slurton Slime Boards. The smooth surface also displayed a colorful picture of an unpleasant-looking slug. It bore sharp fangs and had bulging, bloodshot eyes that dangled from the ends of red eyestalks.

They watched the girl maneuver the board expertly back under her feet and land smoothly in the grass.

Kase grinned in admiration. "Wow! Did you see that?"

It hadn't taken the kids of the city long to figure out that the slime trails behind the slug buses could make for excellent sport. Soon an entire culture had evolved around sliming. Inevitably, it hadn't taken much longer before countless brands of slime boards and new clothing styles were available at stores all over the city. Every kid in every neighborhood just *had* to have a board.

Fortunately, the slugs didn't seem to care. Lately, however, there had been a rash of unfortunate accidents when oncoming slugs had squished riders as they jumped from one slime trail to another. Luckily these accidents were very rarely life-threatening. Most of the time, a rider was simply out of commission with aches and strains for a few days.

Kase loved to slime and was planning to get himself a new board from one of the bigger manufacturers. *Maybe a Slurton,* he thought, *just like that girl's.*

Murdox looked up at Kase and sort of smiled, like a dog sometimes does. He often forgot that Kase was just a kid.

Murdox thought about Brent Hobskin and smiled again in his doggy way. Kase's father had been Murdox's partner in the Incantation Enforcement Agency when the two of them had created the Counter-Curse Division. It must have been about five years earlier when they were on a routine case together, involved in rooting out some trolls who had recently taken up residence in the sewage tunnels beneath the city. During their investigation they had found a section of deserted subway tunnels that didn't appear on any of the city maps. Apparently the trolls had converted the tunnels into a shrine to practice outlawed voodoo magic. When the two agents had tried to slip away quietly to report their discovery, some roving trolls who had been hired to patrol the tunnels had captured them.

They had bound Murdox and Brent with ropes, gagged them, and then dragged them forcefully to their encampment. The two agents were roughed up, thrown into a meat locker, and hung upside down for storage. The trolls kept them there for days, forcing them to eat half-cooked meat in a ghoulish attempt to fatten them up.

After they'd been held captive for what seemed like forever, Brent was able to pick the locks that bound them. When the coast was clear, the two agents made a hasty escape from their imprisonment and raced out of the tunnels.

After making it back to the IEA safely, they returned to the tunnels with a heavily armed enforcement squad to capture the trolls and their leader-- a formidable witch doctor. A heated battle ensued, but the enforcement squad finally managed to capture all the trolls and retake the sewer. Brent and Murdox were given the duty of arresting the trolls' leader.

Murdox still shivered with a cold chill each time he recalled that day. The witch doctor was fiendishly evil and frightening to look upon. He wore a huge wooden mask crowned with ebony feathers. It was painted black with streaks of dark red. The outer edge of the ghastly mask was adorned with strange symbols and mysterious runes. Silently screaming shrunken heads had been strung together to form a necklace draped around the witch doctor's neck. On his wrists he wore copper bracelets adorned with more of the cryptic markings.

The two agents had found him hiding in a

deserted tunnel, a good distance from all the action. After a heated battle, they were able to wrestle him to the ground and subdue him with an anti-magic collar. Before they had been able to turn him over to the enforcement squad, however, the witch doctor had broken free, removed the anti-magic collar, and tossed some sparkling dust into the air. Then he'd simply disappeared in a puff of smoke.

The Enforcement Squad had tracked him down again and cornered him before he fled from the tunnels. In a final attempt to escape, the witch doctor cast one last spell, and he targeted Brent and Murdox. The squad placed the anti-magic collar around his neck once more, but not before he was able to utter the final words of his curse.

Fiery blasts of lightning erupted from the witch doctor's fingertips, amplified by the magic bands on his wrists. Brent dove in front of Murdox in a heroic attempt to protect his friend from the spell. The incantation had been intended to transform both men into mindless beasts, but only Brent received the full force of the devastating curse.

Magical energy coursed through his body, painfully twisting and almost turning him inside out. Because Brent had taken the full force of the incantation, he was left stripped of his humanity. In less than a minute, he had been transformed from a man into a wolf. There was no trace of his former self.

For months after the incident, Brent had been tested and treated in every conceivable fashion in an attempt at a cure. In the end there was no hope. Finally he was released to live out the rest of his life as a wolf in a massive park built on the thirteenth level of the city.

Brent Hobskin's sacrifice was not in vain. Murdox's life had been saved by his deed. In spite of Brent's heroic gesture, however, his body was unable to absorb all of the overwhelming strength of the magic. The fierce curse was powerful enough to ripple around Brent's body and affect Murdox, as well.

To Murdox's great dismay, he was physically transformed into a wolf-dog. But because Brent had absorbed the majority of the evil energy, Murdox was only partially affected. The magic had changed his body, but he was able to retain his mind and soul, along with most of his memories. Unfortunately, he also retained his not-so-charming personality. It took Murdox several years to adjust fully to living in the wolf-dog body, but he could thank his lucky stars that Brent Hobskin had sacrificed his very existence to save him.

Since that time, Kase and Murdox often went to the park to visit Brent, but rarely were they able to catch even a glimpse of the elusive wolf. On a few occasions they had spotted him with a small pack of other wolves. They were glad that he seemed happy and untroubled by the world around him.

Kase and Murdox remained lost in their private thoughts as the slug made its way down one of the many city thoroughfares, stopping frequently at traffic lights and trying to avoid the occasional pedestrian. A string of kids tagged along behind the creature, catching a quick ride on its slimy ooze trail. Before long, it reached the vertical train station that served as the central hub for upward transit throughout the city of Cloudview. The city locals simply call the vertical train "the V" for short.

Cloudview was not just an ordinary city; in fact, it was actually several cities in one. Here, technology and magic had grown together. Cloudview was a colossal structure, a hundred levels tall. Each level was actually a city in itself, with an overwhelming assortment of multi-story buildings of every conceivable shape and size. As in every city, the horizon was a mass of towers, spires, domes, and cathedrals that created the cityscape. The tallest of these buildings acted as columns designed to support the next level of the city. The tallest buildings, resting on the highest level of the city, projected more than twenty-thousand feet in the air.

Unfortunately, Cloudview was also tremendously overpopulated. Kase often wondered how so many vehicles and creatures could live and travel together in such a chaotic mess. From a distance the city appeared to be an enormous beehive. Thousands of skyways interlinked the many levels of the city. Each of the skyways was packed with sky cars, transports, and living creatures in a wild assortment of shapes, colors, and sizes. The structures were so massive and the aerial traffic patterns so dense that the sky could sometimes even be blocked from view.

At the V station, the slug slowly eased its way to

the curbside parking and allowed its passengers to disembark. Kase and Murdox climbed off the slug's back and gave the creature a couple of pats of encouragement as they strolled past its bulbous head. This simple act of kindness thrilled the slug so greatly that it rolled its gigantic gooey tongue out of its mouth and licked them both from head to toe. Murdox howled in embarrassment as they both tried unsuccessfully to wipe the green slime from his fur.

The two detectives then made their way through the deep crowds and toward the train station's main concourse. Murdox nearly got them into a fight when he accidentally slammed into a nasty old ogre who smelled of rotten eggs. Fortunately the ogre was late for a train and had to rush off before he could hear Murdox suggest that he would make excellent slug bait.

Kase pulled out his laminated train schedule and studied it. "We can catch the Number Nine train up to our level in a few minutes. It stops a few times, but it will get us where were need to go. We can then take the horizontal the rest of the way to the office. We'd better hurry!"

The two agents quickened their pace, threading their way through throngs of creatures, both human and very inhuman. At their gate, Kase pulled out a couple of coins and dropped them into a turnstile. Then they walked down a breezeway that connected the terminal station to each individual train.

On first inspection, the V looked like an ordinary train. It had a big, black, steam-driven engine with a series of smaller silver passenger cars trailing behind. The only difference between this train and any other train was that it traveled straight up. For ease of loading and unloading, however, the train sat in a horizontal position while stopped at the station.

Only a few other passengers were boarding the train that would take them to the sixty-seventh level of the city. Kase and Murdox boarded and found a couple of seats near the middle of the car. A flashing red sign began blinking: *Fasten your safety harness.* Then an overhead speaker announced, "The train is about to leave. We sincerely hope your safety harness is fastened. The doors are about to close. Please hold on."

The door to their passenger car quickly closed

with a slam, and the train started to rumble forward. The whistle blew, and a billowing white steam cloud shrouded the entire length of the locomotive. In a moment the train picked up speed, and Kase and Murdox's heads were slammed back into the padded headrests.

The train began barreling right toward the back wall of the station. Even though everyone knew what to expect, all the passengers instinctively braced themselves for impact. Just an instant before the gleaming black engine reached the wall, it bolted upright and headed straight up, entering a dark vertical shaft. The engine, with its silver passenger cars trailing behind it, hurtled upward into the city of Cloudview. Its own cloud of steam obscured any details of the tunnel walls as the cars rocketed upward. Everything outside the windows became no more than a smoky blur.

Within a few moments, the train began to slow. Then it dropped back into a horizontal position and rolled forward into the next station. After it jolted to a stop, the side doors opened, and the overhead speaker blared an appropriate message: "The train has reached the Seventeenth Level. Please disembark carefully. Have a nice day."

A few of the passengers got out, while a few more boarded. Each of the new arrivals took their seats and fastened themselves in. Then the overhead speaker announced, "The train is ready to leave this level. The next stop is the Thirty-third Level. If your safety harness is not fastened, the acceleration could smash you like a mashed potato. Thank you for your cooperation."

The doors shut, and the train leapt away from the Seventeenth Level station.

After a few more routine stops, the train reached Kase's and Murdox's station. They unbuckled themselves from their seats and stepped off the train. An overhead sign pointed toward the exit, while another larger sign pointed to the horizontal tube platform. Kase and Murdox made their way through a mass of people and headed in the direction of the horizontal tube.

The horizontal tube platform was known as the HT station, and the trains that ran through the tube were called "HT's". All the levels had similar transportation systems for city commuting. The V train provided upward transport between various levels of Cloudview, while the HT commuted passengers horizontally on a single level. Every HT station in Cloudview was situated at the center of each individual city level. In a hub-and-spoke design, a series of tubes radiated out from each central station, transporting passengers to locations throughout that particular level.

Kase absolutely loved riding public transit around the city levels. He thought it was like going to an amusement park and taking a spin on all the good rides. Murdox did not agree. Like most things forced upon him, Murdox found public transit distasteful.

Kase and Murdox stepped into a bronze metal tube that held about fifteen riders in a standing position. They then walked to the front of the car and grabbed hold of one of the many silver poles installed inside the transport.

Kase flipped over his train schedule and double-checked that they were on the right HT car. "Ours is the last stop for this car… but if we don't get off, we'll have to ride the whole route again."

Murdox seemed uneasy and was already looking

a bit green around the edges. "Don't worry," he retorted. "I'll make sure we get off."

Without warning, the door slammed shut. Then the contraption blasted away from the platform with a loud *whoosh*. Kase clutched the handrail as hard as he could to avoid being thrown to the back of the car, and Murdox wrapped both paws around the bottom of the pole to prevent himself from taking flight.

The HT soon came to an abrupt halt at its first destination. The momentum from the sudden stop flung everyone in the car forward, except for the very experienced riders who knew how to hold on tightly enough. After the less seasoned riders picked themselves up off the floor, several more commuters boarded. In an instant the doors closed again, and the car zoomed away from the platform.

Kase watched through a side window as the city sped by in a blur. "I wonder how fast we're going."

Murdox was just trying his best to keep Ms. Willeby's cookies in his stomach, where they belonged.

Before long--although not soon enough for Murdox--they reached their stop. After they exited the car, Kase had to wait a few minutes for Murdox to regain his balance. When he was ready, they began walking the rest of the way to their building.

Murdox looked quite a bit worse for wear. "*Bleh! I can't stand riding that blasted thing.*" He belched. "I think I'm going to be sick."

"Come on, you big sissy… let's get a move on." Kase peered upward. "The moon is about to rise, and we don't want to be outdoors when that happens!"

Out of the corner of his eye--just beyond the edges of his vision--Kase sensed, rather than saw, a creature scaling up the side of a nearby building. Then they heard a distant, unearthly howl that put a definite spring in their steps.

Kase tried again to see the sky, but it was almost impossible. A dense cloud of commuter traffic blocked his view. For a brief moment there was a break in the mass of vehicles, and he could see darkness setting in.

Actually, what he was seeing was only an artificial rendering of the sky, projected onto the ceiling of this level of the city. The overall consensus during the construction of Cloudview had been that the enchanted ceilings should mimic the outside weather conditions. Generally speaking, the city founders felt that a sky would be much more appealing than a mass of concrete blocks. Unfortunately the engineers of the city got carried away and took this concept a bit too literally. When it rained outside the city, it also rained inside the city. If it snowed, sleeted, or hailed on the outside, the artificial sky mimicked every weather phenomenon that Mother Nature could throw at them.

As he pondered the artificial weather, Kase steadied himself against a brisk breeze that blew up a cloud of dust. Another eerie howl brought him back to reality. This world was a very dangerous place to live. The throbbing vibrations and warmth of the city drew in all types of nocturnal predators like moths to a flame. To the predators' pleasant surprise, they found that they could prowl inside the city as easily as they could in the outside world. It was common knowledge that it wasn't a very good idea to be caught outside at night without serious protection.

Kase and Murdox walked down a small, dark passageway. They crossed through a poorly lit tunnel and then stepped out into a pool of artificial light radiating from an overhead street lamp. There they hesitated for a moment, admiring the familiar sights.

Through the thinning overhead traffic, thousands of twinkling lights began illuminating the sky as the early evening approached. Towering buildings lined the narrow street as far as they could see. Some of them appeared to defy the laws of physics, leaning and bending at the strangest angles according to whatever whims the designers had. At the end of the street, an enormous building rose all the way up to the artificial sky. The light of a rising moon was reflected in its cobalt blue windows, giving the appearance of a shimmering waterfall.

Kase and Murdox walked the short distance to their office building. At the entrance they stepped between two enormous winged creatures, chiseled in slate-gray stone. Kase had never actually determined what species they were, but he had a strong feeling that he didn't wish to bump into any of them in the dead of night.

Passing cautiously between the statues, they

reached the glass doors that granted them access to One Wizard Place.

55

-Chapter Three-
The Incantation Enforcement Agency

One Wizard Place was the headquarters of numerous government organizations, including the Mystical Bureau of Investigation (MBI) and the Incantation Enforcement Agency (IEA). Kase and Murdox were gainfully employed by a small crossover branch known as the Counter-Curse Division of the IEA. Actually, their office was so small that there were only three employees.

In the past, the MBI and the IEA, along with a few other agencies, had attempted to deal with cases of magic that went astray or curses that had to be undone. Unfortunately, many of the agents who were assigned to these cases became cursed themselves and were often transformed into bizarre creatures of one kind or another.

It wasn't long before the government insurance carriers began dropping their coverage, particularly for on-the-job injuries. For example, it became terribly expensive to compensate a family properly when its breadwinner had been changed into an armadillo.... The IEA powers-that-be decided to develop a separate organization to handle these particular emergencies-- hence the creation of the Counter-Curse Division.

The first of many problems with this division had been that no qualified agents were interested in the job. Along came Brent Hobskin, who took it unto himself to commandeer the new office. His first move was to volunteer Murdox, his friend and partner at the

IEA, to help him run the new division.

The first year had been difficult, but Brent and Murdox had withstood the test of time--not to mention quite a few very close calls. The agency never actually grew in size, though (mainly because no one else wanted to work there), but it did a lot of good and saved the government a fortune in insurance claims. For this reason, the new division remained in existence.

When the former Brent Hobskin--at that point a wolf--took up permanent residence on the thirteenth level of the city, Kase took it upon himself to follow in his father's footsteps. He actually had little choice. He hadn't found a way back to his home world, and he felt that he owed it to his father to keep up the good fight.

*

Once in the lobby of One Wizard Place, Kase and Murdox made their way to a bank of human-sized transparent tubes that disappeared into the darkness above their heads. Kase stepped eagerly into a tube and pressed the Number 99 button on the control panel. In an instant, he was sucked up the tube and was quickly on his way to the ninety-ninth floor of the building.

Following Kase's lead, Murdox climbed reluctantly into one of the tubes. He reached up with his paw to push the same numbered button. Remembering that the tubes weren't designed to transport wolf-dogs, Murdox quickly tilted his snout upward, high above his ears.

Murdox clearly recalled his first humiliating ride in a tube in his present form. He'd been sucked tail-first up ninety-nine floors at a breakneck speed. It had taken a week to prevent his tail from standing straight up from his back end… not to mention all the razzing he'd taken from his peers. Among the many comments he would much rather have forgotten by now were *"Gee, I didn't know you were a pointer!"* and *"Why don't you raise a flag from that pole?"*

The tube hurled Murdox unmercifully up the side of the building, snout first, and spat him out an opening on the ninety-ninth floor.

Kase had been examining a worn spot in the carpet with his face, and started to pick himself up off the floor when the wolf-dog blasted out of tube and nearly landed on top of him.

"I really need to put some pillows on the floor here."

Murdox tumbled to a stop and noisily tried to clear his sinuses. "*Humph!* I wish they would just put in some stairs or maybe even... dare I say an elevator? *Humph!*"

"No way. That ride is awesome! It's nearly as much fun as the HT."

The two agents stepped away from the lift tubes and headed down a long, narrow hallway in the direction of their office. They had just passed through the glass door lettered with *Counter-Curse Division* when Paulette greeted them.

"Welcome back! I see that both of you are still alive and apparently no worse for wear."

Paulette happened to be the very same orangutan who had greeted Kase and his father when they had first arrived in the stairway world. As the administrative assistant, Paulette sat behind a hefty wooden desk and was in charge of the telephones. Most of the time, she pretended not to work for the Counter-Curse Division. This made her feel safe from any stray job-related threats that might follow the two agents back to the office.

Kase and Murdox didn't have to pretend very hard that she didn't work for them, since she hardly did any work at all. Her mornings weren't much more than a series of long coffee breaks, interspersed with personal phone calls, and her extended lunch breaks lasted most of the day. The remainder of the afternoon she used for additional phone calls and errands she hadn't got to during lunch. Kase and Murdox had long since given up trying to encourage her to be more diligent. At this point, they just figured that any work they could get out of her all was cause for gratitude.

At the moment, Murdox was looking at her with an odd expression and then seemed to realize that he had better say something. "I just love the hat. It complements your dress nicely."

Murdox had a hard time keeping his snout shut, and when they first began working together, he had continually made negative comments about Paulette's unusual taste in clothing... but this behavior hadn't lasted long. As he had discovered, to his great surprise, orangutans are remarkably strong for their size. He had made one too many snide remarks about her floppy yellow hats and had been tossed violently across the room. A dent, shaped like his head, still remained in the far wall as a reminder either to be nice or just keep quiet.

The office of the Counter-Curse Division was a modest size and was furnished in a style typical of government workplaces. A few worn wooden benches sat against a pale white wall in the reception area, and a brochure rack stood at the back of the room. It was filled with a collection of pamphlets with titles such as *Just Say No to Casting Spells* and literature on useful topics such as *Coping with Your New Appendages*. There were pamphlets on everything from living as an ostrich to family counseling for your extra head. For the most part, however, there was nothing very special about the office. As Murdox so often reminded Kase, the only color in the room came from Paulette's interesting choices of clothing and her cosmetics artistry.

Kase and Murdox had just sat down when an overhead siren startled them half to death. They looked up at the ceiling and listened as the speaker began sounding an alarm and blurting out directives.

"All available agents must report immediately to the armory for a situation briefing and weapons pickup!"

Kase and Murdox looked at each other in disbelief. As if on cue, the message repeated three more times, and they finally let it sink in. The two agents hadn't even had a chance to rest before they found themselves running down the hall and jumping into one of the lift tubes for a fast ride downstairs.

On the armory level, the building's many lift tubes were dumping agents mercilessly onto the cold marble floor. Kase and Murdox landed in a heap of other agents who had been too slow to get out of the way. Kase found himself looking at a gray-haired rat-man on whom he had happened to land.

"What's going on?" Kase asked him.

The little rat-man was attempting to squirm his way out from under Kase.

"Well, if you would be kind enough to remove yourself from on top of me, maybe we could both find out."

Kase stood up. "Sorry about that."

The boy rearranged his pants and tried his best to smooth out the wrinkles in his shirt as he and Murdox made their way to the armory's security checkpoint. Neither he nor Murdox had any clue as to what was going on. Murdox didn't seem very worried about the situation, though, which made Kase feel a little more at ease.

They joined ranks with a growing line of agents and slowly made their way to the armory's security door. When it was his turn, Kase located his employment identification and presented it to a three-headed guard. The guard checked the badge with gigantic, bulbous eyes that protruded on green stalks from his left-hand head, which then nodded approval to a glass-enclosed brain situated on his middle head. The brain twitched and pulsated within its enclosure, acknowledging that the identification portion of the security check was complete.

Just as Kase thought he was finished, the third head decided to give him a once-over. It sniffed him from head to toe with a huge, moist nose that tickled and made him laugh out loud. Finally the guard seemed satisfied and allowed the embarrassed boy to pass through the checkpoint into the armory.

All of the agents were ushered into a conference room, where they each grabbed a folding chair from the batch that had been stacked neatly against one of the walls. The agents arranged themselves in an orderly fashion and then sat muttering amongst themselves.

When it looked as if everyone had arrived, a tall man dressed in black riot gear stepped to the front of the crowd. Kase knew him as the commander of the Enforcement Squad Division. This was the publicly known policing division of the IEA that was in charge of enforcing the law by extreme measures. Historically speaking, some creatures on this world needed a bit of extra coaxing to follow the rules. This was not to say that the IEA was a militant organization, but when the likes of your enemy were three-hundred-pound ogres or seven-feet-tall trolls whose only form of communication was a club over the head, sometimes a show of force was necessary.

One Wizard Place also housed a number of

covert Special Operations agencies that were not so publicly known. Their actions were kept very secret, and when they were called upon, some very serious trouble was typically brewing.

"Ladies and gentlemen, thank you very much for your prompt attendance. I will get to the point immediately. For those of you who do not know me, I am Commander Devin Crashblade, and I am in charge of the Enforcement Squad Division."

Kase looked him over. He was a tall, muscular man who had black hair with silver streaks running through it. His dark, penetrating eyes scanned the audience with complete confidence. This wasn't a guy you'd want as your enemy! Kase had heard through the grapevine that he was a tough man to work for but was extremely competent at getting the job done.

Crashblade went on. "It has come to our attention that a militant group calling themselves the Ogre Nation has savagely besieged and is currently attempting to infiltrate the Gold Trust Financial Institution, located on the fiftieth level of our fair city." He paused for a moment and gazed out at the crowd, allowing the information to sink in before going on.

"We have deployed squads in the hope of breaking this siege, but due to the recent troll uprising, our full strike numbers are very low, and our injured list is very high. As agents of the MBI and the IEA, you have all been combat-trained to deal with such unfortunate events. I am asking you now if I may call upon volunteers to assist us in bringing down this raid."

Immediately after the brief speech was concluded, almost everyone else in the room began muttering to each other and anxiously asking questions. In his customary calm, cool manner, the commander fielded the questions and responded.

"Details of the robbery are trickling in as we speak, but it is safe to say that there are approximately 150 heavily armed ogres and at least 75 equally armed trolls."

Agents began asking more questions and making comments, and he went on.

"Yes, I am aware that neither the ogres nor the trolls have enough intelligence to have devised this scheme. We have been investigating a clandestine organization that is apparently the brain-trust behind these attacks. We are fairly certain that the recent troll uprising and this attempted break-in are somehow connected, but at this moment that is not our utmost concern."

That was more than enough to get the group's blood boiling. Nearly everyone in the room had known someone who had gotten hurt during the troll uprising, and they were all ready for some payback.

The room again began to rumble with mutterings, and again the commander listened intently to all the questions and answered them as accurately and promptly as he could.

"At this moment we are primarily concerned with stopping this robbery. Without a doubt, this group requires financial support to bankroll their operations. We feel that stopping this raid with a strong show of force will slow the progress of whatever or whoever is behind all these attacks. Suffice it to say that we are working on a few good leads, but at this point it is in our best interest to stop their movement here and now."

An agent who looked like a tiger in a suit stood

and spoke his mind, summing up the overall sentiments of the group. "Just start handing out the ammo, and tell us what to shoot at!"

This got the crowd cheering.

The commander smiled and pressed a small button on a remote transmitter that was hooked on his shirt pocket. The wall behind him slowly rotated open and brought into view a vast chamber behind it.

"Find what you need in the armory, and report to the roof for transportation. The enforcement squads and local security are holding off the ogres at present, but it won't be long before they will need to fall back for reinforcements."

The armory chamber was enormous. Kase could hardly see from one end of the cavernous room to the other. The most impressive aspect of it was that it appeared to contain every conceivable implement of war ever created.

Kase and Murdox watched as other agents in the room made their way into the armory. In an orderly fashion, a team of attendants received the group and started handing out some serious artillery. Then riot gear and fragment-proof armor was fitted and handed out to all the agents, regardless of their shape or size.

For the most part, agents working for the MBI and the IEA were Bipeds--at least most of them walked on two legs. After all, the majority of this world's population were two-legged creatures of some sort. This was not to say that all of them were humans; more than half of them were not. There didn't seem to be much rhyme or reason to the size or shape of each individual, but most seemed to be primarily of mammal or reptile descent, whether they walked on two legs or four. Of course, a lot of the inhabitants of the city had been irreversibly altered into the forms they now had by some magical means, but many of them were simply born that way.

Kase watched with fascination as a jackal-woman was fitted with dark gray fragmentation armor, more commonly known as a "frag suit." She looked cool and collected, as though this sort of thing happened to her every day.

Standing next to her was a grizzly bear who was putting the finishing touches on his camouflage riot gear. With the help of an attendant, he strapped a crisscrossing bandoleer of heavy ammunition across his gargantuan chest. The bear was then handed a massive assault weapon that Kase recognized as a Gatling gun. This lethal weapon was designed to create a continuous stream of projectile firepower. It was essentially a five-barrel cannon designed to rotate rapidly as long strips of ammunition were fed into it.

The massive creature hefted the weapon with ease and swung it in Kase's direction for effect. Before Kase could react, the bear heaved the weapon over his shoulder and winked at the boy to indicate that he meant no offense. Still, that sight wasn't something Kase would soon forget. His startled expression probably gave the bear a good, silent laugh.

Murdox watched as the efficient volunteers assembled their gear and prepared for the battle ahead. Nervously he made a sort of gulping sound as he looked up at Kase. "Let me guess. You missed getting combat training."

Sporting a big stupid grin, Kase stammered, "Well... the first time it was offered, I missed the first week of class because we were out on assignment… and I guess I just sort of forgot about signing up for any other classes."

Murdox stared up at him with a not-very-pleased expression on his face. "I suppose I can't talk you out of this… but at least let me give you a crash course tonight. Follow my lead, and listen to everything I have to say."

Kase started to retort but still visualizing the bear, thought better of it. "Don't worry, I'll listen."

"And another thing… I'm sure you've already noticed, but most everyone here still has some variety of human shape, even if they aren't exactly human. I think it's pretty obvious that I'm now a wolf-dog, and what's most important about this is that I don't have fingers or an opposable thumb. The only way I can hold a gun is in my teeth, and that doesn't do me much good if I'm trying to shoot the darn thing. I'm physically stuck in this doggy world of mine. The only reason I still have a job is that we are the only two agents dumb enough to work the Counter Curse Division." Murdox let that sink in for a few moments.

Kase used his thumb and forefinger to mimic a

gun. Speaking in his best cowboy accent, he drawled, "Don't worry, fella. I'll do all the shootin' for both of us."

Murdox barely nodded and then stuck his tail between his legs, suddenly feeling a bit woozy.

Kase was soon fitted with a green frag suit that wasn't nearly as heavy as it looked. The attendant handed him an armored helmet with a visor that could display a heads-up view of vital armor-and-weapons statistics. To his pleasant surprise, it could even display in an infrared mode so that he could see in almost total darkness. The attendant then handed him a couple of slick pistols to try out for size and weight. Each could fire an electrostatic energy blast that would render an ogre unconscious with one shot. Of the two, Kase chose the Berrington Model 12, simply because it looked snazzier.

Kase took a look at his reflection in the mirror that hung in the fitting area. *"Cool!"* he commented, striking a menacing pose.

Murdox gulped and went looking for some equipment for himself. With Kase's help he managed to find an odd assortment of armor that he and the boy were able to strap around his canine body, yet which still allowed for some freedom of movement. Murdox figured that if he couldn't carry a weapon, at least he could protect himself from being shot. As he turned his attention back to Kase, who was still fumbling with his new blaster, it occurred to Murdox that the ogres were the least of their troubles. Although he realized that neither of them had any intention of getting into the heat of the battle, he also knew that somehow things didn't usually work out quite the way they intended.

Finally equipped with high-tech battle gear and the jumbo blaster, Kase and his well-armored canine partner fell into line with the other volunteers and headed for the roof.

On the rooftop of One Wizard Place sat three rugged-looking troop transports, each capable of commuting two dozen combat-equipped personnel anywhere in the city at any time. The manufacturer of the aircraft had officially named it the Dragonfly because of its four narrow wings. The general consensus, however, was that it looked more like a bloated bumblebee.

The craft had a sloped nose, which came to a point in a black nose cone, and round, yellow-tinted windshields on either side of the cockpit that looked like big bug eyes. The fuselage of the aircraft was slightly oval and narrowed to a flat tip at the tail. It had two sets of long chocolate-bar-shaped wings mounted to the top of the fuselage in an H-shaped design. At the far end of each wing was an independent, rotating engine pod, capable of powering the craft in a vertical takeoff configuration. Once the craft was aloft, each of the four engines provided more than enough thrust for normal flight characteristics.

The tail end of the craft was lowered down and provided ramp access into the open cargo bay. Twelve red nylon seats, facing inward, lined each side of the fuselage, and there was a central rack designed for weapons storage.

Kase and Murdox boarded the craft and grabbed two seats near the forward bulkhead so that Murdox could chat with the pilots. Within moments, the remainder of the volunteers boarded the craft and found seats after stowing their weapons efficiently in the center rack. Kase watched all of this in awe, wondering how he was going to get his own weapon into the rack without accidentally blasting someone.

In preparation for flight, the pilot closed the aft troop door and reported that they had been cleared for takeoff. Then, with a powerful rumble, each of the four engines came to life as the last of the volunteers strapped themselves into their seats. The ship swayed slightly with a rocking motion as the craft lifted away from the rooftop, leaving a cloud of dust in its wake.

The captain reported from the cockpit that the other two ships in their convoy had already lifted off and were well on the way to their destination. It would take an estimated fifteen minutes to reach their drop-off point, where they would rendezvous with the other vessels, at which time a member of the Enforcement Squad would meet them and assign each of them a duty based on their individual experience. Murdox looked over at Kase again and hoped that meant guard duty for the troop transport, but he doubted they could be so lucky.

The craft lifted higher into the sky and slowly

began to merge into the seemingly endless stream of traffic. Kase was watching the traffic flow through the forward windscreen.

"What if no one will let us onto the skyway?"

The captain responded with a sly grin. "Well, we've got a pretty loud horn to honk, and the co-pilot says he's awfully good at obscene gestures. But if that doesn't work, there's always the particle cannon mounted to the belly of the craft."

Just then, seemingly on cue, the pilot slipped the ship effortlessly into the stream of traffic and made the final course adjustments for their rendezvous point.

*

The Gold Trust Bank was a veritable Fort Knox. The bank itself was situated in the center of a high-walled compound with a number of smaller flat-roofed administration buildings surrounding it. Located in the four corners of the outer wall were observation towers with artillery cannons designed to ward off unwanted intruders.

Currently, three of the cannons were billowing black smoke and appeared to be out of commission. The last working tower was under heavy siege by a group of well-armed ogres and an enormous mountain troll. The troll was pounding away at the base of the tower with a spiked wooden club, while the ogres were using assault ropes to scale the structure. The Enforcement Squad had managed to keep them at bay while preventing the assault from reaching the main bank complex, but the ogres and trolls seemed to be advancing on the weakening group.

From the air, Kase and Murdox watched the heated battle. Bright red and green blaster shots filled the smoky compound as heavy artillery rained swathes of destruction around the unprotected buildings. The two other transports had already dropped off their troops, who were rapidly being deployed into the mayhem.

The maze-like layout of the smaller administration buildings prevented an aerial assault. It would be far too difficult to use aircraft to attack the trolls and ogres without harming the Enforcement Squad troops. The commander was correct--the strike would have to be limited to a ground incursion. This strategy would also prevent any unnecessary damage to the bank itself.

The Dragonfly made a quick approach to a landing zone located behind the main complex. Without shutting down the engines, the pilot dropped the craft onto the tarmac and quickly opened the aft cargo door. Each of the volunteers grabbed his or her weapon and shuffled quickly down the exit ramp. Following Kase, Murdox barely had a chance to leap off the ramp before the pilot throttled up the engines and lifted away from the landing pad.

As promised, a member of the Enforcement Squad was waiting for them and quickly assigned a team leader for each of them to report to. He explained that the ogres had taken the front half of the compound but were being held at bay by cannon fire and current troop deployments. There was little time before the last cannon would fall and the ogres and trolls would reach the surrounding buildings. It was up to the volunteers to place themselves in specified areas to prevent access to the bank itself.

The Squad member displayed a map for all of them to look at and briefly detailed the many access points that needed to be guarded. Fortunately all the administration buildings funneled into one main channel that led to the bank itself. By positioning certain teams in key locations, it was believed that the Squad should be able to end the assault quickly. Until then it had merely been a numbers game--the ogres and trolls had simply outnumbered the Enforcement Squad.

In record time the volunteers from the three transports had been assigned various locations to protect. Kase and Murdox were given the relatively easy assignment of guarding one of the smaller side buildings that housed the air conditioning and environment systems for the bank. Murdox was relieved to see that this building was far away from the main battle and that it would be very unlikely that the assault would make it to their location.

The two detectives stood patrol outside the door to the small metal building. Nearly an hour passed, and the battle seemed to be waning.

Kase could discern only faint sounds from the

distant warfare. "I haven't heard much gunfire in the past fifteen minutes. I think maybe this thing is going to be over soon."

Murdox had been listening intently at the door with his head cocked when Kase spoke. "Quiet down, pickle-head," he snarled. "I think I hear voices coming from inside the building."

"I don't hear anything but occasional gunshots."

Murdox rolled his eyes. "How many times do I have to remind you? I'm a dog… my hearing is just about a bazillion times better than yours. I think we had better check this out."

Kase cautiously depressed the latch, opened the door to the tiny building, and peered inside. They both entered the small structure, and Murdox looked around carefully.

Murdox sniffed at the floor and listened again. "It doesn't sound like the voices are coming from in here, but from below us."

The little building was a pumping station for a steam ventilation system that supplied heated air to the bank. Numerous green and red tubes ran in various directions from the main pump in the center of the room and down into the floor.

Murdox found a small access door in the floor that appeared to lead to the underground steam tunnels. "It sounds like the voices are coming from down here. Open the door, and we'll check it out."

Kase grabbed hold of the floor hatch handle and heaved it open. A narrow circular staircase dipped downward into the darkness below them, giving Kase an eerie feeling of déjà vu… but he let it go.

Murdox quietly led them down the metal steps and paused when he reached the damp floor below. Low-wattage bulbs provided minimal lighting to the tunnel, which housed the same red and green tubes running in both directions for as far as they could see.

Murdox cocked his head to the side, and looked down the passageway to the right. "The voices and a nasty smell seem to be coming from this way."

A draft blew through the passage and Kase scrunched his nose. "Yup, I smell it too."

Murdox sighed and led Kase down the passage in the direction of the smell. After about five minutes, they could see where the path veered off to the left. Just as they came to the corner, they heard the voices again and dropped to the floor. Crawling forward, the two agents cautiously peered around the curve. There, ten ogres were standing no more than a hundred feet away.

They were appalling creatures, covered in filthy gray-green flesh and each weighing about 250-300 pounds. They had shaggy black hair and beady little eyes set deep in their swine-like heads. Each had pointy overgrown ears, a snout for a nose, and two sharp tusks protruding upward from his lower lip. They all carried massive assault weapons that struck fear in those on the business end of the barrel.

For the most part, ogres were used as cheap mercenaries. They were not endowed with much intelligence but could be bought easily and could certainly put up a good fight when they chose to.

"Stupid humans! They never would have suspected that we would sneak into the bank from an underground tunnel. We slipped in right under their little noses."

Murdox reacted quickly; "Kase, use the communicator in your helmet and call for backup immediately. We have to get out of here, now."

The ogres had already smelled them, and quickly bounded around the corner to try to blast the eavesdroppers. Murdox realized just how close the vile creatures were, and pushed Kase ahead of him as they ran as fast as they could back to the pumping station.

The ogres were firing rifles at them, blasting huge chunks of concrete and mortar from the old tunnel walls.

Fortunately for the two agents, ogres aren't very good marksmen to begin with, and the complexity of their powerful weapons made them worse than ever. One of the misplaced projectiles slammed into an overhead pipe that then exploded in a swirling cloud of hot steam, completely shrouding Kase and Murdox from view.

The hail of gunfire continued from behind them. With four legs, Murdox could easily outrun Kase but opted to stay just behind him so he could urge him along. Murdox realized that the frag suit would protect the boy from near misses, but a direct shot from one of the rifles might take him out.

Kase tried feverishly to communicate with the ground forces above them, but running for his life pursued by a mob of angry monsters was distracting him from getting the communicator to function properly. He was fumbling with the armband switches and yelling into his headset, but it was full of static, and he couldn't figure out if he was on the wrong frequency or if this was simply because of their underground location.

"Help... help! This is Kase and Murdox. We're trapped in the steam tunnels and being chased by ogres." He repeated this over and over until someone finally responded.

A monotonous voice came over the headset. "You've reached the operator... can I help you?"

The voice repeated, "You've reached the operator... can I help you?"

Kase responded, "Who *is* this?", distracted by the commotion behind him.

Slightly irritated, the operator replied, "You've reached the operator for the Incantation Enforcement

Agency. How can I help you?"

Kase was dumbfounded. Somehow in his haste he had found the channel that automatically dialed an operator at One Wizard Place.

He ran as fast as he could while trying to explain the situation to the person on the other end of the line. The next thing he knew, a fiery orange bolt of energy slammed into the back of his helmet, blasting it right off his head. It knocked Kase forward, and Murdox slammed into him from behind.

Another of the many stray shots from the ogres managed to blast a power conduit for the tunnel lighting, and the little bulbs started flickering on and off.

Murdox grabbed Kase by the back of the neck and shook him.

"I'm all right… I'll be all right," Kase protested sluggishly. "The blast just blew my helmet off."

Murdox looked down at the smoldering helmet, scarred from one end to the other, and couldn't believe the boy's luck.

"You're lucky to be alive! That shot only grazed you. The helmet saved your life!"

The intermittent lighting and the haze of the hot white steam made them both dizzy. Then another misplaced shot exploded above their heads, bringing them back to reality. Kase wobbled to his feet, and they took off running again. Without his helmet and night-vision enhancements, Kase could hardly see anything in the flickering light of the steamy tunnel. He hoped the operator had understood him and was relaying the message to the ground forces above them.

Suddenly the tunnel ahead of them branched in two directions.

Kase was panting from the exertion of running. "I don't remember a fork in the road."

Murdox looked back at him. "There wasn't one. In the haze we must have run right past the stairway that led to the surface. From the sound of our pursuers, I don't think it's a good idea to retrace our steps, do you?"

Kase rubbed the back of his throbbing head, not feeling the need to reply. They stopped for an instant and contemplated which way to go. The fork to the right seemed to be sloping upward but leading away from the bank directly above them. Murdox thought he could see light coming from that direction.

"I'm sure they're heading for the bank, but you and I both know we don't stand a chance in a head-on confrontation with those guys. We aren't going to do anyone any good if we both get killed, so I say we make a dash for the light and hope it leads out of here. We can find help and cut them off at the other end."

Kase nodded in agreement. He had to rely on Murdox's instinct and night vision anyway, and the light at the end of the tunnel might be their only fighting chance.

The two of them sprinted into the right branch of the tunnel, fully aware that their pursuers were close behind them.

The ogres stopped when they reached the fork in the path. One of the creatures in the lead stuck his dribbling wet snout in the air and sniffed in the direction of each of the tunnels.

The ogre roared eagerly. "They went to the right."

The largest and most menacing ogre of the bunch ordered, "Thrag, you and Flang go after those two. The rest of us will get to the bank before anyone else stops us."

"You'll just take all the gold for yourselves," said Thrag and Flang, almost in unison.

The heavily scarred leader took his blaster and shot it at the feet of the two protesters. They muttered a few choice words in return, but the guns pointed at them by the other eight ogres helped convince them that this sounded like a good idea.

*

Kase ran until he thought his heart had been ripped from his chest. "I have to stop," he sputtered, panting with exhaustion.

Even Murdox sounded a bit winded. "We're almost there. I can smell fresh air."

Kase could also tell that they were nearing the end of the steep tunnel, which had sloped upward more and more sharply. Then, almost without realizing what had happened, they reached the end of the line. The tunnel ended abruptly at a metal gate near the far wall of the compound, but still within the bank's boundaries.

It was late in the evening, and artificial light shone in from a nearby lamppost. Unfortunately, the gate was locked tight. Kase took out his blaster and fired away at the lock, but the weapon he had chosen fired an electrostatic energy blast designed to overload the nervous systems of most creatures and knock them unconscious. To his great displeasure, it had no effect on the heavy metal locks. The gate glowed with blue static electricity as Kase fired his weapon at it over and over again, but the lock simply wouldn't give. Murdox had another idea, though, and dragged Kase back down the tunnel.

*

The two ogres made their way cautiously up the tunnel in the direction of the light. They were not in much of a hurry. They had gained entrance to the steam tunnels from the opposite end of the compound through a similar entrance, and according to the map their boss man had provided, there was a locked gate at the end of this branch of the tunnels.

Thrag and Flang reached the end of the tunnel, but couldn't find their prey anywhere. Even with their meager intelligence, they figured the two fighters they were chasing couldn't be packing much heat or they wouldn't be running.

Thrag smacked Flang in his gut with the butt end of his weapon and growled. "Fool, your overstuffed belly slowed us down, and we lost them!"

Flang snarled back and slammed his boot down on his cohort's foot. "Not me, you gimpy, old troll-bait. It was you who couldn't keep up with me."

The two ogres stared each other down for a few tense moments, but decided it wasn't worth the fight. …It would be more fun to take out their frustration on the closest inanimate objects they could find. They stamped their feet and howled at the ceiling, swinging and firing their weapons wildly.

Red-hot blasts of energy slammed into the walls, knocking huge chunks out of the thick concrete. When that didn't satisfy their lust for destruction they turned their weapons onto the gate, hoping they could blast it open and hear the satisfying sound of twisting metal. The metal bars and lock smoldered under the barrage of heavy weapons fire, but the strong gate and padlock held up against the big guns.

Somewhat satisfied by the destruction they had created, the two rancid creatures gave up and let the dust settle around them. With a shrug they turned and walked back down the tunnel, stopping to examine a few shipping crates that somehow survived their onslaught. Grinning knowingly, they walked away from the crates, then stopped about twenty feet from them.

With wicked laughter, they both suddenly pivoted on their heels and opened fire on the wooden boxes. The massive firepower obliterated the crates and sent splinters flying in every direction. From the heavy use, the guns began to overheat and jerk in their hands. Consequently a few shots missed their mark and blasted the gate again, finally breaking the lock free.

*

Murdox had noticed the wooden crates just

before arriving at the gate. He had hoped that Kase's weapon would break the lock, but as soon as he got a good look at it, he knew he had better come up with another plan. That was when he'd spotted the small ledge above the shipping crates.

By climbing on top of the boxes, he and Kase were able to crawl onto the ledge. Fortunately for them, it actually extended fairly deep into the wall, and they were able to conceal themselves even better than he had hoped. When the ogres had arrived at the gate, the two agents quietly crawled back along the ledge and were able to get a fair distance behind the stinking beasts. Murdox had originally planned on hiding on the ledge, but he knew ogres well enough to realize that they would smell the two of them eventually and they would be sitting ducks on top of the ledge.

When the ogres opened fire on the shipping containers, it gave Murdox and Kase a chance to drop quietly down to the tunnel floor behind the rancid creatures. Their new position allowed Kase to get a clear shot and blast the two ogres with his Berrington Model 12.

Normally one shot would have dropped even an ogre, but Kase wasn't about to take any chances. He let loose a hail of fire like there was no tomorrow. One of the ogres went down immediately, but the other was wearing heavy defensive armor that protected him from the blast. Kase, however, continued firing at the creature, forcing him to stumble backwards. As the ogre fell back, he fired his own weapon into the ceiling, blasting free a huge sheet of concrete that slammed down on him, instantly knocking him unconscious.

*

Kase and Murdox bounded over the fallen ogres and bolted out the broken gate. They quickly found their way back to the main complex of the bank. When they ran up the central steps and into the main atrium of the bank, Commander Devin Crashblade stopped them short. He calmed them down and explained what had transpired in their absence.

With the help of the reinforcements, the Enforcement Squad had managed to stop the ogres in the external assault at the Gold Trust. They thought their job was completed, but then a strange call came in from a frantic operator at headquarters. She explained to the commander that she had received an odd message from a secure headset channel.

On that information, a very battle-weary team of agents had checked blueprints of the compound and located every access point that could be reached from the underground steam tunnels. It turned out that the enemy was occupying three of the five tunnels they located.

Someone had obviously gone to a lot of trouble in devising this plan. In all, they captured nearly forty ogres sneaking around in the steam tunnels.

As best the commander could figure it, the ground attack on the Gold Trust was nothing more than a well-devised diversion. The assault itself had been designed to weaken the Enforcement Squad and keep them from detecting the real plan. While the outside assault was being waged, a well-armed team of ogres had infiltrated the steam tunnels and were to wait there until the fighting stopped. When the coast was clear, the ogres would break into the bank from beneath, rob it clean, and be out again with no one the wiser.

The commander explained that this plan had apparently been prepared well in advance, most probably with the aid of a bank employee. He had the suspicion that there was still someone, or possibly a small, well-funded group, behind all of this, and that person or persons had done the majority of the planning. This was simply too complex of a job for the dim witted ogre's to come up with on their own.

Commander Crashblade congratulated Kase and Murdox on uncovering the plot and saving the day. Once he had gotten word about the steam tunnels, it had been a piece of cake to trap the ogres in the tunnels and capture the lot of them.

Kase and Murdox both knew full well that it was luck that had them literally stumble upon the real plot. They tried to say as much to the Commander, but he only congratulated them some more and commended them for their modesty.

The job of uncovering the masterminds of this plot was far from over, but fortunately for both Murdox and Kase, another department of the IEA would be handling that.

The weary investigators soon climbed aboard a waiting Dragonfly and headed back to the office.

-Chapter Four-
The Great Forest

It was late, and a dim glow from under the office door of the Counter Curse Division caught both Kase and Murdox by surprise. Apparently Paulette, their trusty office assistant, was still there. For a moment they wondered if she might be working late, but just thinking about that made them both laugh.

They entered the office with their curiosity

evident on their faces, and spotted her with a load of office supplies under her arm and an already half-filled shopping bag on the floor. Before they could question her, the telephone started to ring.

With a self-conscious grin, Paulette dropped the load of filched supplies behind her desk and answered the phone. She then delivered one side of a conversation that didn't seem to go anywhere and hung up the phone again. Without saying a word to the detectives, the flamboyant orangutan strolled casually to the kitchen for a cup of coffee.

Kase and Murdox waited patiently for her to return but finally gave in to her bad manners.

"What was that call all about?" Murdox demanded.

The orangutan stepped out of the kitchen while continuing to stir her coffee and ignored his question, directing her conversation to Kase. "Oh, I almost forgot. It seems that the Elf King of Greylok has been turned to stone. You and Murdox need to get to him as soon as possible."

Kase was dumbfounded, shaking his head and

looking to Murdox for feedback. "Wow, this is a new one for us," he mused.

The wolf-dog was busy riffling through the office supplies on the floor but finally took a moment to look up and respond. "I guess it's better than getting shot at by a bunch of stinking ogres, but I'm too tired to think about it tonight. After this evening's festivities, I'm not quite ready to jump right back into the saddle."

"Well… when do you think we should get on this one?" Kase inquired.

Murdox gave up on the pile of pilfered goodies and sat down in the middle of the room. "I doubt that it matters to either one of you, but no one actually knows how to find Greylok. Not that it will stop us, but these kinds of cases can also be very tricky."

Kase was sincerely worried. "Oh, that's not good."

Paulette decided this was the opportune moment to stuff the remainder of her stolen goods into the bag and stick it under her desk. When she was finished, she filled in the two agents with the rest of the information. "Well, don't worry your furry little heads. I've got the directions to a spot where an official guide to their city will meet you. As far as saving the king, that's *your* job…. I just answer the phone."

Kase knew what Murdox was thinking about and stared him down while gesturing at the dent in the wall. The big wolf-dog got the point.

Kase sighed. "Come on, partner. Pack some stuff, and let's get going."

Murdox yawned, barely able to keep his eyes open. "Hold your horses, Trigger. Let's get some rest and get an early start in the morning. We can hardly travel the city at night; it's just too dangerous."

Paulette chimed in, "I hate to agree with Mr. Personality, but he's right. I just read in the *Tribune* that the howlers are getting more aggressive. There's been at least six confirmed attacks within the last two weeks."

Kase remembered the eerie wail from earlier that evening. "I guess you're right. I'm a bit sore from today, anyhow."

"It's agreed, then," said Murdox. "We wait until morning and get right to it. Now all I want to do is grab a quick bite to eat and get some rest."

Paulette swallowed her coffee in one gulp, grabbed a notepad from her desk, and hastily drew up a simple map.

She placed the map on the water cooler and headed for the door. "It's a shame you two don't live in the building next door like I do. I suppose you'll just have to sleep here tonight."

When she was gone, the two agents yawned and found a cozy place to rest for the evening… that way they could make an early start of it.

* * * *

The next morning they woke with the sun and began packing their supplies. Murdox dumped a load of goodies on the office floor, and Kase stuffed them into his backpack. The wolf-dog then grabbed the map Paulette had hastily drawn for them the evening before and studied it. According to her directions, they would need to travel from the office to the ground level of Cloudview, at which point they were to arrange for transportation to a town located at the edge of the Great

Forest. There, a guide would find them and take them the rest of the way to the city of the elves.

Even this early in the morning, the skyways surrounding the metropolis were bustling with traffic. For the most part, though, they experienced an uneventful trip to the base of the vast city.

The buildings that made up the lower level were physically immense, as it was their purpose to bear the load of the entire structure above them. This was also intended to be the primary hub for transportation and inner-city support. In practice, the sheer multitude of people who frequented the lower level and the maze-like architecture of the buildings attracted some of the more nefarious denizens of the population.

This was the definition of a 'low-rent district'. Gangs and hoodlums stalked the vast shadows and poorly lit alleys between the buildings, waiting for lost travelers to round the wrong corner. Rumor had it that even darker and more dangerous dwellings had been built underground, but few agents of the IEA had dared investigate these places. For the most part, it was generally considered a bad idea to stray from the main transportation plazas when traveling to the ground level of the city.

Kase wondered about this as he and Murdox traveled through the foundation of the city, but he was brought back to reality by the wolf-dog. Murdox was looking up at an electronic billboard.

"Let's try to catch the first trug to the Great Forest."

Kase raised an eyebrow and looked over at his friend. "Um… and what might a *trug* be?"

Murdox smiled the way a dog sometimes does. "Well, I guess you haven't been introduced to the half-train-half-bug better known to the locals as a 'trug.'"

Kase shook his head.

Murdox began his tale, "If you want to connect point A with point B by railroad, the terrain normally needs to be flat and level so that a track can be built. Many years ago, the city engineers realized that conventional trains were just too slow and cumbersome to work well outside the city--not to mention that it would require a tremendous capital investment to establish such a railway network, especially in the wilder areas. Thus the trug was invented. A trug is a giant, multi-legged mechanical bug that runs over the ground like an enormous centipede. The benefit is that the trug can run up and down hills or valleys without the need for paved roads or rails. In addition, trugs are big and fast enough to ward off any unwanted attacks from the local predators."

Kase interrupted, "Local predators…?"

Murdox just grinned and led the way down to the station without responding to the query.

After studying one of the many information boards, Murdox was able to locate the appropriate platform for outbound departures. In addition, he learned that only one trug ran from the city to the Great Forest, and fortunately, they were just in time to catch it.

Following the directions on the board, Murdox guided Kase through the terminal building, saying, "Come on, we only have a few minutes to catch our ride, and I want a seat near the dining car."

Just as Murdox had described, the trug looked exactly like a giant metal centipede with windows. It was being refueled when they arrived at the platform.

Kase hesitated at the ramp, not really eager to step into a giant metal bug. Without waiting around for the boy, Murdox stepped off the platform into the mechanical beast. Kase took one final look at the machine, shrugged his shoulders, and followed behind his friend.

Kase found the experience a little disconcerting, but he knew he hadn't been swallowed when he stepped through the entrance door and saw a conductor collecting tickets. Kase handed his ticket to the conductor who, after a quick scan, showed the boy and the wolf-dog to their seats.

Kase had just gotten comfortable when the metal contraption began to vibrate and whine as the engines started to spool up. After a few seconds, the machinery smoothed to a more rhythmic hum.

Murdox was looking out the window, unconcerned. "Here we go," he said.

The giant mechanical creature started to lurch forward. One after another, the many mechanical legs slammed into the soft ground beneath them. Then the machine began to move faster and faster. Surprisingly, it was a very smooth ride, and Kase now understood why

Murdox wasn't complaining too much about this form of transportation.

As the giant mechanical bug really began to accelerate, they passed through the transportation plaza of the city and onto the open plains. Within moments the landscape outside seemed to blur as they traveled at an incredibly fast speed. In less than fifteen minutes, the city had been left behind in the dust.

Kase glanced at Murdox. "Nothing in this place moves slowly, does it?"

Murdox grinned and watched the blurry landscape as they sped across it.

* * * *

By early afternoon, the Great Forest came into view. Kase couldn't believe his eyes--the forest was much bigger than he had imagined. This world had some strange, unearthly sights, but the sheer enormity of this forest was beyond anything he had ever seen. Its name simply didn't do justice to the size of the trees.

As best as he could judge, the largest tree trunks

must have been more than a mile around at their bases. They climbed so high into the sky that their tops were shrouded in the clouds, which only added to the mysterious quality of the forest. A light gray mist drifted among the branches of the enormous trees, creating deep, dark shadows that made Kase feel small and insignificant. He dearly hoped that his wolf-dog guide knew where he was going.

"Pretty impressive, wouldn't you say?" asked Murdox.

Within the hour, the mechanical creature closed the distance to the forest and quickly approached a small town built within the shadow of the trees. The trug began to slow as it approached its destination. Kase looked for his friend, but Murdox had wandered off a few minutes earlier.

Kase wanted to let Murdox know they were close to their stop, so he went looking for him. He found him in an adjoining car, arguing with the conductor. Apparently the wolf-dog had stolen someone's lunch right from a table and had run off with it, leaving the conductor to intercede with the angry passenger.

Kase was in no mood for a major altercation, so he paid the man for his stolen lunch, apologized to the conductor, and promised that it would never happen again. Meanwhile, Murdox had gotten hungry halfway through the scolding and had already wandered away again.

Kase found Murdox checking out another passenger's meal and shook his head in frustration. He grabbed the wolf-dog by the collar and shoved him out of the trug just in time to prevent any further wrongdoing.

Kase glared at his errant partner. "You're impossible sometimes... are you ever *not* hungry?"

"Dog... remember? I'm a dog, I'm always hungry."

The boy stared him down. "Just try to control yourself."

Kase then took a quick look around the town to try to determine what to do next.

"Come on," he told Murdox, "We have to find our guide and get to the King before his condition gets any worse."

The picturesque town was wedged into a clearing at the edge of the immense forest and had been set up to entice tourists from the big city. It was small and easy to navigate, so the two agents did not have much trouble getting around… but being surrounded by enormous trees gave them an eerie feeling.

Murdox looked up into the giant trees that loomed over their heads. "If just one of these fell, it would take out the whole town."

"Thanks for pointing that out."

They had no luck finding their guide, and Murdox was still complaining of being hungry. Kase looked around at all the tourists feeding their faces and agreed that it would be in everyone's best interest to get the wolf-dog's stomach filled. He spied a pub at the edge of town and decided that would be a good spot to grab a bite to eat.

The Lion's Tooth was typical of a back-country pub; the wood paneling was dark, the atmosphere was a bit smoky, and the locals looked at outsiders less than warmly. But the place was clean enough, and Murdox wasn't about to complain when food was involved. They took a small booth near the door and ordered a couple of apple ciders and roasted beast sandwiches.

Neither had gotten a chance to take a bite of food when they noticed that a thin wisp of a man wearing drab green clothing had somehow materialized in the seat next to Murdox. He had light skin, long, shiny, black hair, ebony eyes, and visibly pointed ears. Kase was amazed that somehow this elf was managing to scratch Murdox's head and distract him from his meal without even a rumble of disagreement from the wolf-dog.

The man smiled at both of them and began to speak softly. "I apologize for not finding you sooner, but I have just arrived in town myself. My name is Asher, and I will be your guide to the kingdom of Greylok. If you please, we must make haste to the King. His condition is deteriorating rapidly. Please finish your meal, and we can be on our way."

Kase pondered how this guy was able to recognize them for who they were but decided to put the matter aside for a later conversation. He had a ton of questions to ask, but figured that it would be best to get a move on before much more time elapsed.

Murdox got a whiff of his meal and was brought back to reality. Without skipping a beat, he lapped up all the food and his and Kase's drinks before anyone else noticed. Kase grabbed a few last morsels of food and shoved them into his mouth before Murdox had a chance to swipe them, too. The small company then paid the bill and headed for the door.

The elf seemed to glide along in front of them leaving no trace of his passing.

He looked back at the two agents as they rounded the building, and anticipated their next question. "Our transport is just behind the building," he told them. "We'll have to hurry, as it will take us several hours to get to the city." He shook his head in despair. "When I left the king his condition was stable but beginning to show signs of worsening. Unfortunately, I'm not privy to how this might have happened, so I won't be of any help on the matter. …My first priority is to get the two of you to the castle as quickly as possible.

In the interest of time, Kase and Murdox decided against grilling him further, being satisfied that the elf guide had told them all he was going to, for now.

The three of them walked around the back corner of the pub and found a small, grassy clearing. They were only a few feet from the massive trunks that marked the edge of the Great Forest, and the two agents stared at the trees in awe. In the middle of the clearing stood three mammoth squirrels, gathering nuts. This would normally have been an alarming sight to Kase, but the huge squirrels somehow seemed proportionate to the size of the big trees.

Murdox, however, was whining and howling in fear.

Kase looked at the quivering wolf-dog. "What's the problem Murdox?" Then he realized what Murdox was staring at and grinned from ear to ear.

The squirrels had saddles on their backs. These were their rides to the city.

With great difficulty, Asher and Kase then strapped a very reluctant wolf-dog to the back of a squirrel and tightened down the ropes until the elf seemed satisfied.

Kase approached his squirrel and raised his left

leg, squeezing his foot into a leather stirrup. He then hoisted himself up, swung his right leg over the back of the beast, and tried to situate himself in his saddle as comfortably as possible.

Asher was scratching his own squirrel affectionately behind the ear. "Please, don't either of you worry a bit. These creatures know the woods better than I do. I'll bet they could scamper across it with their eyes closed."

Kase decided to test his riding abilities. He grabbed hold of a set of worn leather reins and cautiously tapped his heels against the animal's sides. The squirrel stopped gathering nuts for a moment, leaned back on its haunches, and rotated his head nearly all the way around to look at Kase.

Asher was grinning at the boy. "Don't worry… they'll follow me when the time comes. You two just hold on and enjoy the ride."

Murdox gave his squirrel a sniff and started to whine again.

Kase scooted around in the saddle and looked up into the trees. "How long a ride is it?"

Asher shook his head as he looked at the quivering wolf-dog. "It's not far--no more than a few hours."

Murdox whined a little louder. Then Asher spoke a strange Elven word, and the lead squirrel dropped his nut to the ground and scampered straight up the nearest tree. Kase followed close behind, atop his own squirrel. Murdox, looking utterly distraught, let out a thunderous howl as his mount followed in their wake.

It was an amazing ride. Up, up and up the three squirrels raced, ever higher into the trees. The wind whistled and whooshed across Kase's face. The only thing that could have made it more fun would have been if Murdox hadn't been howling so loud. Even so, Kase decided that this was probably the best ride he had ever had. All he could see to either side were the deep brown trunks of countless trees, but every so often he would catch a glimpse of the green forest canopy through the mist that hovered far above him.

Asher looked back to check on the progress of his companions. He had to yell to overcome Murdox's terrified howls.

"We should be reaching the lowest branches of the trees soon. When we are high enough, we'll level off and head in a northbound direction to Greylok."

Soon they were deep into the mammoth branches of the great trees. Asher's squirrel dropped down onto a huge branch that extended horizontally like a highway into the distance. He patted his animal and waited patiently for the other two to catch up. Within moments Kase's squirrel hopped onto the branch next to the elf. The young boy was grinning like a Cheshire cat.

Murdox's squirrel landed with a thud only a couple of minutes later. Murdox himself was strangely silent; his unnerving howls had stopped when they reached about halfway up the tree. When they realized why he was so quiet, Kase and Asher couldn't help but grin. Apparently, he had fainted dead away.

They checked to make sure he was all right and then decided to let sleeping dogs lie, so to speak.

Asher looked far ahead into the trees. "Follow along the branches with your eye--they actually link up and form a crude network of roads. We have used these treetop highways for centuries to travel across the forest undetected."

Asher's squirrel dashed off along the branch into the distance. Kase and Murdox's squirrels followed right behind. The boy was having the time of his life. His squirrel leaped and vaulted from branch to branch in a death-defying acrobatic performance. Half the time Kase's stomach was in his throat, particularly when he looked down.

The leaves of these massive trees were so dense that Kase rarely spotted even a glimpse of the sky through the tangle of branches far above his head. Up and over branches, down and around obstacles, his squirrel bounded from limb to limb in a mad dash across the treetops. Kase barely kept his lunch down when his squirrel suddenly leaped sideways and then planted itself in a gravity-mocking pose to avoid an unseen barrier that got in its way. Even this couldn't wipe the smile from Kase's face.

Before long the forest began to look more organized, and the treetop commuting became easier. The branches were growing closer together, creating something like a superhighway beneath the squirrels' feet. The forest canopy was gradually looking more civilized. The tree trunks grew to form natural tunnels and bridges, all intended to link the forest into one massive plane. This natural platform soon became wide enough to allow small huts and forts to be built amongst the branches. Eventually these became homes and buildings, seamlessly carved into the dense bark of the trees.

An immense goshawk with great golden wings swooped down low to check them out. Another elf straddled the bird's back and was steering the beast right at them, but the rider soon recognized Asher as a friend and allowed the company to pass. Asher smiled and waved to the sentinel as he and the two detectives passed below. The hawk soared silently back up to its lofty place of concealment, ever-vigilant for new arrivals.

Here they passed more and more travelers on their journey into the city, and Kase realized that riding squirrel-back was commonplace for the elves. Soon the branches they rode on had grown together completely into a solid wooden platform that spanned outward as far as he could see. Asher guided them onto a main thoroughfare, and they merged into a veritable traffic jam of treetop commuters.

Massive towers and freestanding buildings had been raised on the wooden plane, and an immense city in the trees soon towered before them. It had been constructed seamlessly within the forest canopy, blending so perfectly into the trees that it wasn't apparent where each tree ended and the next structure began.

Kase was amazed that for countless generations this marvelous city had remained hidden from the rest of the world.

Elves of every shape and size were going about their daily business, completely oblivious of Asher and his new friends. Squirrels were not the only types of transportation the elves used. They ranged from cat like to spider like creatures, but all seemed competent in traversing the branches with ease. A few elves were lucky enough to fly on the backs of colorful songbirds, which danced among the branches and warbled cheerful songs.

The canopy above their heads began thinning, allowing sunlight to flood between the branches, and they could see the sky again. Kase marveled at the sights as the small company traveled through the city and into the downtown district. He gazed wistfully at the tightly packed buildings and crowded streets, wishing he could explore the many shops and restaurants that lined either side of the road.

Gradually the urban sprawl gave way to more stately manors, constructed on large, open plots of the wooden plane. Asher continued to guide them through beautiful suburban neighborhoods until the road became a narrow lane that wound its way into a grove of aspen trees. They followed the lane through the trees until it suddenly opened onto a perfectly manicured lawn that spread out before the three riders. Down the center of the lawn, hedged by neatly trimmed bushes, ran a cobblestone path that led straight to the King's castle.

It was just as Kase had imagined… a gleaming white stone castle complete with parapets, towers, and a drawbridge. The bridge was lowered, and the group crossed over a moat of crystal-clear water. A trio of brightly colored fish swam over to see who was crossing overhead, but after a brief examination of the visitors, the fish swam off to investigate a much more interesting bug that had landed with a *plunk* a short distance away.

Once across the drawbridge, the group stopped at the main entrance to the castle. Four elves in flashy velvet uniforms, armed with long staves, helped Kase and Asher dismount from their squirrels. They carefully pulled the unconscious Murdox from his saddle and laid him gently on the ground. With a sigh, Kase dug a hand deep into his backpack and pulled out a zip-lock bag containing a giant T-bone steak, which he waved slowly under Murdox's nose.

The wolf-dog's nose twitched and sniffed at the slab of meat. Suddenly, he snapped at the steak and sucked it into his mouth. After gulping it down, he said casually, "So sorry to have nodded off on you guys. I guess that ride was just so relaxing it must have lulled me to sleep."

Kase and Asher glanced at each other and smirked.

The elf guards were becoming agitated.

"We must hurry!" said one. "The King's condition is deteriorating by the moment."

The guards quickly led them into the castle, where they passed through a vast, arched hallway draped with elaborate tapestries.

The finely loomed panels recorded the history of the elves. The interwoven designs depicted hard-fought battles to claim the Great Forest. They detailed not only the military strife but also the immense undertaking of the construction of the city and the castle. At the far end of the hallway, the images gradually changed to scenes of far-off lands and special places the elves wished to immortalize.

Kase and Murdox were in awe as they were led up a flight of polished stone steps and into a vast chamber completely enclosed by glass. A river flowed into the room and cascaded into a deep pool of blue water. Long flowering vines and exotic plants luxuriated in the warm environment, and colorful songbirds nested among their leaves. In the center of the room stood the King's bed, carved of an exotic dark wood. Surrounding the bed was a small entourage of attendants who were trying to make him as comfortable as possible.

The guards stepped aside to let the agents pass, and the attendants backed away from the bed as they saw Kase and Murdox approach. The two agents carefully pushed aside the delicately woven draperies attached to its upper frame.

A tall, elderly man with long, white hair and purple robes rose from a chair placed next to the bed. As he stood, the old wizard tripped over his long robes and staggered into the side of the bed.

"Oh, thank the Forest Mother, Herself... you have finally arrived." On his head was an enormous pointed hat that drooped over his eyes and which he was desperately trying to keep from covering his face entirely. "I'm Enob, the High Wizard to the King. Please... can you do anything for him?"

Kase helped the elderly wizard move away from the bed while Murdox began to examine the king. It was apparent that a sort of creeping paralysis had immobilized the monarch.

The King was tall even for an elf, well built and very distinguished looking. He wore his white hair long in the traditional style. The King looked up at Murdox with green eyes that reflected his wisdom but were distinctly clouded with pain. His skin seemed to be graying, and his entire body felt stiff and cold.

The two agents poked and prodded at the King's hardening skin. Kase grimaced, glancing over at Murdox and shaking his head.

Under the watchful eyes of the court, they quietly discussed their options. Kase dropped his backpack to the stone floor and reached deep into its confines. He withdrew a few dusty old spell books and finally chose a large leather volume with gold trim. It was titled: *101 Incantations from History's Greatest Alchemists.*

Kase turned to the wizard, who was ringing his hands. "Tell me, how did this whole thing come about?"

The old wizard seemed to shrink visibly. He tugged downward on his floppy hat until his eyes were hardly discernible from beneath its folds. In a shaky voice, he tried to explain what happened. "I really don't know, honestly… but from what I can tell, it was just a horrible error. I was in my study, putting together a potion that would transform flowers into stone. You see the Queen had seen a flower sculpture on a recent trip to the city. Her Majesty found them exquisite, so she requested that I try to create one for her. Later that afternoon, while working on the Queen's request, I was informed that the King had been complaining of a headache and had requested a remedy to help ease the pain. I can't imagine how it might have happened, for I have never done such a deplorable thing before.... Somehow I must have confused the ingredients and mixed them together."

By this time the poor old wizard was almost crying. He was utterly devastated by his unfortunate mistake and had difficulty finishing his tale. An exquisite elf maiden then approached the old wizard and laid her hand on his back. She was tall and slender and wore a green velvet dress that complimented her magnificent shiny black hair. Her sea-green eyes shone with tears of grief as she spoke in a gentle elfin voice. "Oh, pooh! I just can't allow this to continue. It was I who requested that Enob manufacture the potion to turn the flowers into stone." She hesitated for a moment.

"But you see, I had a far more devious plan for this potion."

Kase and Murdox looked at each other in disbelief. Assuming that she must be the Queen, they wondered how such a fair lady could have been responsible for such a treasonous act?

Once again she hesitated and looked about the room to each face in the small crowd. Then she gathered her composure and continued. "I just couldn't stand it anymore. It was that cat!" The Queen's beautiful face was now scowling, and she pointed to the end of the bed.

Everyone looked at the fat, orange-and-black-striped cat whose tail waved gently over the feet of the King.

"I resented that cat… always so snuggly with the King--I sometimes believed His Majesty loved him more than he did me." She continued in the same vein for nearly a minute before she realized that she was getting carried away.

"Well, anyway, the King didn't have a headache--that was simply a ruse I created. I needed an excuse to get into the wizard's study so I could get my hands on some of the potion he was creating. When the wizard was out of sight, I pocketed a small bottle of the concoction. I was feeling so jealous that I had intended to slip it into Fluffums' milk--that's the cat, of course. I just thought it would make him less cuddly."

The Queen smoothed her hair and continued. "Poor old Enob had no idea of my intentions. He returned with the headache remedy and placed it into a similar bottle for me. I insisted that I would give it to the King myself, so he instructed me in how to administer it to His Majesty in his afternoon tea." She blushed deeply with shame. "Honestly, I was the one who mixed up the powders. I can't believe my stupidity, but I was the one who actually served it up to my husband with honey and a twist of lemon. I didn't realize my mistake until it was too late!"

The Queen looked around the room at the shock on everyone's faces and then began to weep quietly. She paused for a moment to glance around again, then began to sob uncontrollably.

She fell onto the King's chest, weeping into his

stiffening robes and crying, "How can you ever forgive me?"

It appeared that a huge weight had been lifted from the old wizard's shoulders. Within a few moments he regained his dignity and looked years younger. Even his hat seemed to sit on top of his head more securely.

Kase didn't know what to think about the accident. He was glad that this horrendous incident was simply a misguided mistake and not some twisted plot to do away with the King… although the circumstances were awfully underhanded, especially concerning the poor cat.

Murdox, on the other hand, had no problem with the treacherous plot--he was a wolf-dog, after all, and didn't care much for cats. Trying to make extra points with the Queen, the wolf-dog nipped at the cat's dangling tail, scaring him off the bed.

Kase glared at Murdox. "I'm glad we got to the bottom of the *whodunit*, but we still have to figure out how to cure him."

Something suddenly occurred to Enob, and he excused himself from the room. He hastened off to his study to retrieve the ingredients he had used to create the incantation. When the wizard returned, he and the two detectives reviewed the incantation thoroughly, comparing Kase's book against the old wizard's library notes. But the book and the notes all said the same thing… that this incantation would be very harmful to humans.

Murdox shook his head and muttered, "…a little late for that."

"*Duh!*" said Kase. "But what are we supposed to do if it is used on people?" Kase dug into his pack and pulled out more spell books. Finally he found an answer in the last book of incantations. He read the text aloud for all to hear: "To counteract various incantations that have gone awry, please refer to the text *Alchemy Undone, Compiled to Remedy the Spells of 101 of History's Not-so-great Alchemists*." He looked up from the book. "Apparently, a book was written for just such emergencies."

Kase read further and then waggled his finger. "Aha!… For pricing and availability, contact Wizard-Wide Publishing at 888-555-7799." Then he remembered something and took another long look into his backpack, muttering, "Here kitty, kitty, kitty."

Suddenly realizing what he was saying, he popped his head out of the backpack and looked in the Queen's direction. "Sorry, I didn't realize what I was saying. It's just a dumb old expression."

The Queen simply blushed, and Kase resumed his search for the book.

"Whew! Found it. Always be prepared, that's my motto." Kase looked squarely into Murdox's eyes. "Shush… no comments from the peanut gallery." He pulled the book from his pack, opened the dusty tomb, and flipped to the section on spell reversals. He quickly found the reference to this particular incantation and ran through a long list of ingredients for Enob to gather.

To their pleasant surprise, between the agents and the wizard it seemed like they had all the ingredients they needed… except one. When Kase spoke the words aloud, a hush fell over the crowd.

"What… what did I say? We need a talon from the right front foot of a blood dragon. I don't have one in my bag… do you?"

Enob shrunk back into his robes, pulling his hat down over his eyes. No one else answered either.

Finally Murdox looked up at Kase and cleared his throat before speaking. "You see, Kase, there are only two blood dragons alive on this world at any given time. They are the fiercest and most feared of all dragons. I seriously doubt that anyone who has actually seen one has ever returned alive to tell the story, much less leave its lair with a souvenir like a talon."

Kase looked worried. "It's not looking so good for the home team, is it?" He continued to flip through the book and then shrugged. "I guess we'll just have to go get one ourselves. So, how exactly do we find one of these guys?"

Kase looked out over the crowd, but nobody would meet his eyes.

As he read further in the text, Kase found another passage that caught his attention. "We'd better hurry. From what it says here, we have precious little time before the spell becomes irreversible. Not counting today, it looks like we have only about ten days before it's too late!"

"Wait just a second!" said Enob. "I'll be right back." He quickly slipped out of the room again and hastened to his study. He returned carrying a long, dusty metallic tube under his arm. He unscrewed the top of the container and gingerly withdrew an ancient map that was slightly yellowed and frayed at the edges. "I knew this would come in handy one day!"

The old wizard laid out the map carefully in front of them.

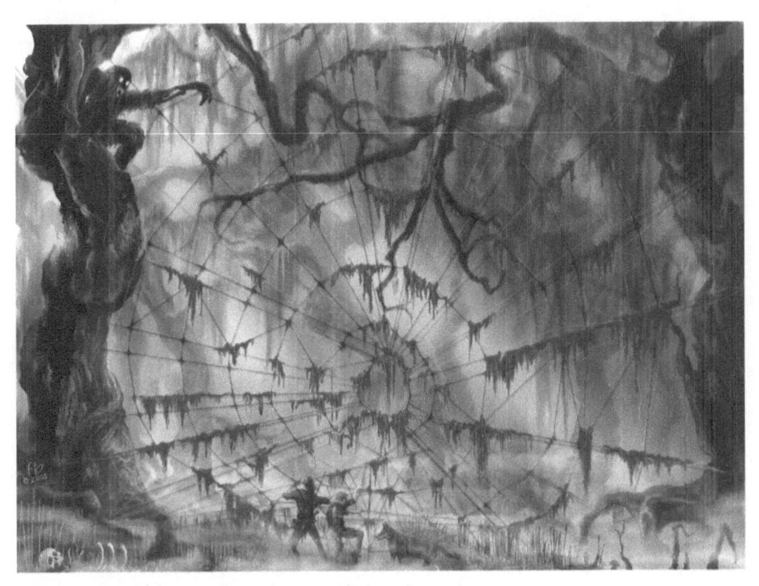

-Chapter Five-
The Swamp of Doom and Despair

K ase, Murdox, and Enob gathered around the polished wooden table where the wizard had laid the weathered old map. The King's attendants allowed them some elbow room and turned their attention back to the patient. For the next several moments, the little group studied the ancient drawings intently.

Murdox groaned. "This is sheer lunacy. If facing a blood dragon isn't bad enough, how are we ever going to get there and back in time to save the King?"

Kase looked down at the wolf-dog. "I guess we'll just have to do it quickly."

Murdox snorted, "Gee, I never thought of that… sure am glad you're here with all those great ideas."

Enob waited for the bickering to stop and pointed to a spot on the map. "According to this ancient Elven text, it is said that a female blood dragon lives far to the north, deep in the Badlands of Moog. Her cave is situated within a treacherous mountain range known as the Dragon's Spine. Another such dragon, presumably a male, lives far to the south on an island in the middle of the Fire Sea."

Murdox rolled his eyes. "Well, don't those just sound like great little vacation spots?"

Kase began to measure the distances on the map. "Right. Well, which do we choose? They both seem about an equal distance from here."

Asher, who had remained silent up until then, made his way quietly to the table. "I have traveled far and wide over this world and would humbly wish to add some of my own advice."

"By all means," replied Enob, with nods of encouragement from Kase and Murdox.

"The Fire Sea is treacherous in any season, but during this particular time of year the seas are far too violent to cross. Vast, devastating firestorms rage across the open ocean, burning and destroying anything in their path. Even if we could procure the right ship, no one would dare captain it. I dare say that I don't have the capability for such a task. In my opinion, the Dragon's Spine is the lesser of the two evils."

Kase beamed with enthusiasm. "That's good enough for me."

The Queen, who had slipped in quietly behind the little group, had been listening intently. "That sounds like as good a plan as any to me," she said. "I shall prepare a legion of our finest soldiers to thwart this beast and return with its claw."

Murdox was the first to reply. "I can't believe I'm even saying this, and not that a full brigade of crack elf commandos wouldn't come in handy… but that just won't work."

Enob thought about what the wolf-dog had said and agreed. "Murdox is correct. Dragons are by far the most intelligent and magical creatures alive on this world. The blood dragon species is the fiercest and most powerful of them all. Even the weakest of their kind could smell that many soldiers from miles away. Only a small, clandestine party of two or three people would stand a chance."

Without a second thought, the Queen decided their fate. "Well, then, it's settled. You shall leave immediately. Asher will accompany the two of you on your adventure. He is one of our finest rangers, and you will most certainly be needing his protection."

Murdox whimpered. "But... but I didn't mean *we* or, in particular, *me*."

Kase patted him on the head. "Did you really think we could get out of this?" Murdox growled at him.

The Queen appeared to be greatly relieved now that a plan was in place. She glided gracefully over to the King and kissed him on the head. Then she made her way back to Murdox and scratched him behind the ears.

She appeared to have completely forgotten that this whole mess was of her making. Without looking back, she strolled casually out of the room, mumbling something about going shopping.

Dumbfounded, Murdox, Kase, and Enob watched her leave.

"Well, I guess that's that," said Kase.

As they all began to walk out of the room, a frail voice called to them from the bed. Everyone rushed to the King's side. He stretched out a cold, stony hand and slowly reached for Murdox, gently patting him on the head.

In a raspy voice, the King said, "Thank you for your selfless sacrifice on my behalf. I trust you will return safely. For this deed you shall be greatly rewarded." The King slowly pulled his hand from Murdox and lay it carefully back on his chest.

Asher said, "Rest now, my King. We shall return safely and with good fortune."

It seemed that the King had also made up his mind about their fates. Still a bit overwhelmed by all that had just occurred, Kase and Murdox were led from the room and taken to guest quarters. Both of them needed to get some rest.

Asher and Enob remained behind to make final preparations for the journey. It would be on their shoulders to plot the shortest route to the dragon's lair. Unfortunately, on account of the King's critical condition, safety would have to be compromised to make the best possible speed. It was essential that their trip be completed within ten days to prevent the King from becoming a very large paperweight.

After a short rest, the party gathered at the front of the castle and made final preparations for their journey. Before they departed, the Queen made sure they were well supplied for their long journey, and Enob gave them his maps to help guide them on their course. Fortunately, there were still many hours of daylight remaining when the small party took to the trees. Once again they rode upon the swift squirrels that had brought them earlier that day. Murdox put up a pretty good fight about it, but in the end he was convinced that this would be the easiest way to travel.

Thus, with a hastily prepared plan and enough

supplies to last them for ten days, Asher led their small company through the vast expanse of the Elven kingdom. A small contingent of guards escorted them away from the castle and a short distance into the deep woods. Once the last of these riders was left behind, the small band was on their own. Kase and Murdox again found themselves high above the ground, speeding swiftly from tree to tree on the ancient highways that had grown into the upper canopy of the Great Forest.

Hours passed, and remarkably, Murdox remained conscious.

Finally, he could take no more. "We've been riding for hours. I'm exhausted!"

Asher turned to the small company. "We should reach the edge of the Great Forest within the hour. There, I promise, we will drop to the forest floor and make camp for the night."

It didn't take long for the forest to be cast into deep shadows as the sun slipped below the horizon. Shortly after sunset, just as Asher promised, the small party came to the last of the great trees. Without the aid of the sun, it was pitch black under the forest canopy. To

Murdox's complete horror, the squirrels suddenly began clawing their way headfirst down to the forest floor-- which was the last thing he remembered about that part of the trip.

Murdox awoke sometime later to the sound of a small fire crackling not far from where he lay. He looked up and could just barely discern the shadowy outlines of the three squirrels that were resting quietly just beyond the fire's glow.

Kase and Asher had just finished a light meal and were preparing to get some sleep. After stumbling around for a few minutes, Murdox found the food Kase had prepared for him. He spotted the boy crawling into a warm sleeping bag only a few feet away. "Thanks for the grub."

Kase nodded and silently watched him eat.

They were camped in a small grove of aspen trees that bordered the Great Forest. The evenings were still fairly warm this time of year, and Asher hadn't felt it necessary to create an extensive shelter. The thin, gray-white aspens hardly obstructed their view of the stars shining on this cloudless night, so the small fellowship of three found themselves staring silently into the dark sky.

Murdox finished his meal and looked over at Asher, who was slipping into a light bedroll. "So, tell me what fun you have in store for us on this trip."

Kase glanced at him and smirked. "Feeling better after getting something on your stomach? You must have fainted from hunger pains," he said with a laugh.

Murdox ignored him and repeated his question to Asher.

"I have traveled these lands my whole life. I know them well enough. Enob and I were able to glean the shortest and quickest path to the Dragon's Spine, but I must say that 'shortest' is a relative term. The journey will not be easy."

Listening intently, both Murdox and Kase swallowed with difficulty. Kase was the first to speak. "So, what exactly do you mean by that?"

Asher sat up in his bed and withdrew the ancient map from his pack. He held it within the fire's glow so that they could both see what he was explaining. Asher pointed to their approximate location. Then he located a series of mountains drawn at the northern edge of the yellowed map.

"We are just about here, and we need to be there." Slowly he began to trace their route with his finger. "By early morning we will be beyond the realm of the Elvin Empire of Greylok and on the border of the Swamp of Doom and Despair."

Murdox stole a worried glance at Kase. "I've heard that name before, but I thought that it was simply called the Swamp of Doom. Where did 'Despair' come from?"

Asher offered a dark, toothy smile. "Only recently have I read about this in your city's newspaper. Apparently Doom alone did not do justice to the great number of… let's just say *misfortunes* that have occurred in that vile place. Adding Despair to the name seemed fitting."

Kase worried as he recalled the details of the newspaper story. "Yeah, I remember reading about that, too."

Asher looked at both of them. "Assuming we're able to pass through the swamp alive, we'll have a short journey to the Ocean of Sand. There we'll have to charter a vessel to make the dangerous crossing. Upon its far shores, we will be in the Badlands of Moog, where we'll gain a foothold into the Dragon's Spine."

Murdox whined. "Well, doesn't *that* just sound like a pleasure cruise...."

Kase had taken the map from Asher and was using his fingers to measure the distance between the locations Asher spoke of and to figure how far they'd already come.

The Elven Ranger watched Kase for a moment and continued. "If we were to follow a safer route, we would never get there and back again in time to save the King. This, unfortunately, is our only option."

Kase had to agree, with what he could tell from the map. Then an idea struck him. "You know, it just occurred to me... why can't we fly there? I saw elves flying on the backs of birds in Greylok. We could probably even have commissioned a Dragonfly and a couple of pilots for the assignment."

Murdox glanced over at Kase and shook his doggy head. "I was waiting for that question," he replied. "I know that we don't travel too far from the city very often, Kase, but the farther you get away from the city, the bigger and meaner the predators get. In Greylok, under the protective canopy of the Great Forest, short flights are possible and relatively safe. But one step outside the protection of the forest or the city, and the dragons and giant raptors rule the sky. We would instantly become a tasty snack for them. Even an armored Dragonfly wouldn't be a match for one of the giant predators. It would probably just irritate the creature to pry open the craft to get to the soft meat inside."

Kase didn't enjoy the reference to soft meat and let the subject drop. As if on cue, an ear-splitting roar thundered across the night sky. A massive shadow eclipsed the pale moonlight. Not far from their camp, the trees rattled and shook in distress as some poor creature fought a losing battle.

Asher looked in the direction of the sound. "We aren't the only ones eating dinner tonight."

Kase's eyes grew wide, and he pulled his sleeping bag up to his nose. "I guess that totally clears things up. Don't mind me if I cry out during the night in a panic-induced nightmare. Thanks for answering my question, though."

Cushioned by the fallen leaves and soft grasses of the forest floor, the three of them pulled up their sleeping bags tight and after a long while slid into a deep sleep.

* * * *

The next morning, a light rain began to fall. Cloaked and hooded, the small party unceremoniously gathered up their gear and packed for the day ahead. Before long, they were riding at a good pace across the forest floor on a soggy but fairly well-marked path.

Wishing to make the most of their time, they rode through the early hours of the morning and ate a light meal as they traveled. Their haste paid off, and by mid morning the forest began to give way to more marsh-like conditions.

A light, damp mist hung in the air. The surrounding bog boiled and burbled, belching out foul odors that drowned their spirits. Damp and chilled, they trotted on. Kase was amazed that Murdox didn't complain, even when the rain had thoroughly soaked through their heavy cloaks.

By mid afternoon the rain lessened--and the hazy mist slowly began to burn off. What appeared to be strange shapes in the mist gave way to gnarled and twisted trees, heavily draped in soft mosses. The narrow, damp path stretched onward ahead of them for as far as they could see. To either side, oddly shaped vegetation grew from the slime-covered waters of the swamp.

The Swamp of Doom and Despair was extraordinarily silent. All they could hear was the sloshing of the squirrels' feet in the muddy path beneath them. Then a heavier mist began to roll in. It gradually became more difficult for the sunlight to penetrate the thick foliage surrounding and concealing them. Before long they could see little but the strange, hazy shapes of the trees about them.

Murdox contorted his head so that he could get a better look around. "Well… if it wasn't for the stench, this place might not be quite so bad."

Asher was listening intently in the eerie silence for any sign of unwanted company. "Stay on the path. We must keep in sight of each other. Soon the waters of the bog will deepen, and it will be easier for the nastier denizens of this foul place to track us."

Kase was taking a good look around, too. "Exactly what might this place hold in store for us?"

Asher glanced over his shoulder at him. "The usual, I suppose: snakes, crocodiles, giant piranhas, quicksand, and swamp fairies, of course--but I'm not too concerned about those creatures. What frightens me the most is the saber-tooth tree sloth."

Without waiting for the inevitable questions, Asher continued. "They occupy the top of the swamp's food chain. After thousands of generations, they've managed to become more than just eating machines... they've gotten smarter. We have to keep our eyes on the trees. They hide in wait for unsuspecting travelers to cross beneath them, then without warning they drop down from the branches and snatch their victims with very sharp claws. If they catch us off guard, we don't stand a chance. The biggest of them could probably carry off one of these squirrels."

No one said a thing after that, and all eyes were now focused on the trees. The heavy mist gradually thickened until they could hardly see one another, but they continued down the path and deeper into the swamp. A fish jumped out of water in the distance, breaking the eerie silence, and Kase jerked in his saddle.

Murdox grinned. "So, Kase… try your best not to get eaten."

Kase tried to ignore Murdox and relaxed back into his seat. Even though no one would admit it, they all had the same fearful thoughts running through their minds. They were helpless to control the inevitable, so the small party sank back into their saddles and let the mist surround them.

Asher led the way, followed by Kase. Murdox rode at the back of the pack, grumbling about nothing in particular. They rode like this for some time before the muddy path narrowed, and they found themselves surrounded by deep, dark, boggy marshes edged by tall reeds and thin rushes. Ahead of them, black shapes flitted across the path, quickly disappearing from sight.

One of the black, multi-legged creatures dashed headlong directly in front of Asher. It dove into the reeds that were hedging the water's edge, chased from behind by an overfed swamp rat. Momentum carried the two hapless creatures into the bog, and in an instant the water churned violently as they became lunch for piranhas.

The little company unconsciously moved closer to the center of the path and continued on their journey deeper into the swamp. The gnarled trees seemed to move in closer, as if watching them with unseen eyes. A cold, damp breeze brushed through the bows, chiling the adventurers to the bone.

Quietly at first, then more insistently, a soft voice whispered to each of them--reassuring them, reminding them of warm, soft beds and cozy fireplaces. Suddenly everything seemed right with the world. The whispering voice told them of faraway tropical lands surrounded with white-sand beaches and clear ocean waters.

The trail ahead of them gradually branched off in several directions. Entranced in a magical spell, each of them was led slowly down one of the paths. The soft voice was guiding each of them deeper into the swampy quagmire on separate routes.

Kase was led by an unseen force. In his mind, nothing was wrong… actually, everything was perfect. He was reminded of home, when both his mother and father were alive. In his imagination, they were all playing in the front yard of their house. Everyone was laughing and happy. The song called to him, strong and unrelenting. It was pulling him deeper and deeper into its spell.

The same was happening to Asher. He was now happier than he had ever been. No longer did the worries of his station keep him constrained. He was free to travel the world, unbound by duty. Dragged from his awareness were the pressing thoughts of his King and their mission. Only happy, carefree images danced in his well-structured mind.

A swamp fairy casually stroked the damp fur of a particularly rotund, yellow-eyed swamp rat. The fairy stood knee-deep in mud, singing a tasty tale for each of his new visitors--a tale that he hoped would convince them to come on over and stay awhile.

The little creature blended into his surroundings perfectly. His skin was tinted a pale shade of iridescent green from the light coating of moss that covered his entire body. He vibrated gently within the power of his magic. Ever so quietly he sang his magical song, drifting the words over the wind, letting the tune weave its way smoothly through the trees.

Excited by the song, the chubby rat nuzzled close to the fairy. The little man whispered into the rat's ear as he continued to cast his spell. "Soon, little one, we will have an exotic meal." All the while, the dark clouds of piranha churned and roiled the waters behind them.

Slowly, each of the wanderers was drawn into a vast, sticky web that had been strewn across each path. Unaware of his surroundings, Kase soon became entangled in the gooey, slime-coated strands. He thought he could hear Murdox howling in the distance but couldn't quite awaken from the dream. His subconscious mind was struggling for control. Deep down, he knew he needed to wake up, but he was far too happy in the magical world that had been woven into his weary head.

Finally Murdox's howling broke through the dream. Kase forced himself to awaken, but what he found was a living nightmare. He was tangled in a giant spider web. The more he struggled, the more entangled he became. He yelled out for his friends, but he feared that they too had been caught in the trap.

Fortunately for everyone, Murdox had keen animal senses. He knew that something was wrong from the start and did his best to keep his mind clear. Even though his thoughts were being lulled by the siren's spell, he had smelled the swamp fairy in time and had resisted its call. He saw the web just before his own squirrel had become trapped. Fearful for his friends, he began to howl, trying to break the hex that had surely lured them into similar situations. He howled and howled as loud as he could in an attempt to snap Kase and Asher out of the trance under which they had surely been placed.

Asher had also been tricked and snared by a similar web spanning his path. His mind was still spinning in private, happy thoughts... but something was wrong. In the distance he could hear the howling of a wolf. His subconscious struggled to gain control, and his years of discipline and training finally won the battle and allowed him to break free of the spell. His keen elven ears alerted him to the danger, and he shrugged off the fog that clouded his mind. He snapped out of the dream to find himself in a precarious situation.

Afraid that he might be too late to save Kase, he withdrew a long, sharp dagger from his belt. Using the elf blade, Asher managed to slice his way out of his entanglement. He rushed back down the path in the general direction of Murdox's call.

Murdox was also searching. The two retraced their steps in the damp, muddy ground and found where the paths had split. They reunited on the main trail and went in search of Kase. Murdox could hear distant sounds, and they followed the path Kase had taken.

Asher and Murdox followed the squirrel's tracks in the mud. In the heavy mist, the cold, damp air smelled of death and decay. Rotting bones of both animals and men, trapped in shreds of filthy webs, were scattered along their way.

They found Kase's squirrel and freed it from the

webbing, sending it back toward the main path. Then they cautiously approached the enormous web where Kase had been lured and now struggled desperately to free himself.

Kase could see them coming as he tried unsuccessfully to break free. He grunted and called out to them, "About time you two showed up. As you can see, I'm just a tad stuck. Some help would be nice."

They couldn't have been happier to see him, but the heartfelt reunion didn't last long. Although Kase was speaking to them, they hadn't really heard a word he had said. Asher had looked up and spotted movement in the trees. Murdox quickly followed his gaze up into the web-tangled canopy.

They watched the branches overhead, and their eyes grew wide with fear. Slowly approaching from high in the treetops was a creature with bristly, mottled green fur and large, orange eyes. Venom dripped from two immense, razor-sharp fangs that protruded from under its upper lip. Its sharp curved claws sliced into the thick tree bark as if through butter as the creature climbed ever closer to Kase.

Asher was scared, but he managed to marshal his senses and begin cutting Kase free of the web. "These abominations are smarter than I thought," he said. "They must use these webs to help capture unsuspecting prey. I suspect that the swamp fairies get some sort of sick thrill out of helping them catch dinner."

Fortunately for the three travelers, evolution had granted the saber-tooth tree sloth only intelligence and raw strength--it had not granted them speed. Understanding their limitations, the sloths had made a deal with the local swamp fairies. They didn't much like the taste of fairies anyway. All it would cost the sloths was a small share of the bounty.

The vile little fairies would use their siren call to lure unsuspecting prey into the sticky webs, thus saving the sloths having to chase after every meal. Once the prey was captured in a web, the creatures could take their time devouring the victim and then leave the scraps for the fairies. For their part, the fairies would benefit from a much wider variety of foods. Up to now, the deal had worked well for both parties.

The sloth saw Asher and Murdox coming and

hastened its pace. It lumbered to the top of the web, attempting to keep them from stealing its meal. It opened its gaping mouth, exposing a vicious smile full of pointed teeth. The creature did its best to hiss and snarl to frighten them off, but the trespassers would not be deterred. It crawled down the web, working its way from one silken thread to another. It was hungry and wanted desperately to grab its prey before it could escape.

The creature hissed and moaned as it made its way down the web. Closer, closer... it could smell the fear in the little human ensnared by the web. The sloth reached out with a curved claw and swatted at the elf who was attempting to steal its meal, but the furred beast was still too far away to reach him.

Seconds before the creature reached Kase, Asher was able to cut him free. As they all ran from the scene, they looked back at the beast flailing in the web where Kase had been just moments before.

They rushed down the path, stopping to cut Asher's squirrel free before regrouping on the main path. They could still hear the sloth hissing and snarling in fury. At that moment they wanted nothing more than to leave this vile place.

Asher took point and led the company away from the webs and back down the dark, wet path.

The sloth and his cohorts were not about to let their meal slip away so easily. Without warning, a little urchin of a creature jumped onto the trail in front of the three travelers.

It was the same enchanting song. The melody brought the dark waters behind the little man to a rolling boil as the schooling piranhas thrashed in anticipation of a meal. A host of rats joined the crowd and lined up along the edge of the path, swaying in tune with the music.

"Not this time," said Kase as he pulled two pairs of furry earmuffs from his backpack. He put one on his head and tossed the other to Asher.

Asher put the muffs over his ears and grabbed a great wooden longbow that had been strapped to the back of his squirrel. From his quiver he withdrew a wicked-looking black arrow and knocked it into his bow.

The elf pulled back the bowstring, took aim, and effortlessly released it with a *twang*. In what seemed like slow motion, the arrow sailed towards its intended target in a deadly arc.

Thwap. The arrow struck, and the world rushed back into real time. Kase and Murdox turned to watch the swamp fairy, and they noticed that he hadn't been skewered.

Murdox called out, "You missed!"

In the next second, a tree sloth fell into the mud right in front of their feet with a *thump,* a black arrow protruding from its green hide. Asher just smiled at Murdox.

The swamp fairy, who had stopped singing, looked at the fallen creature and breathed a soft "Uh-oh."

In the ensuing excitement, Murdox leapt at the swamp fairy. He grabbed the foul-smelling creature in his jaws and carried him to Kase, who dug into his magical pack and pulled out an enormous birdcage.

"I just knew this would come in handy one day."

Asher pulled from his pack a thin but strong

length of rope, which he tossed in the air and around one of the overhead tree branches. He tied one end of the rope to the top of the birdcage. Murdox stuffed the struggling creature into the cage and shut the door. Hand over hand, Asher raised the cage high into the air and anchored the other end of the rope to a neighboring tree trunk.

Asher looked up at the struggling creature. "I'm sure it won't take you too long to figure your way out of that, but we should be long gone by then."

Carefully stepping around the dead tree sloth, the little company led their squirrels down the main path, which they hoped would take them out of the swamp and away from danger.

Several hours passed as they kept to the path and trudged along through the murky ground. Dark hardwood trees began to take the place of the smaller twisted variety to which they had become accustomed.

Eventually the path widened and allowed for easier travel. They were riding side by side--casually chatting, when something spooked Murdox's squirrel. Kase and Asher looked on in concern as the squirrel took off in a sprint with Murdox holding on for dear life. The squirrel bounded up and down across the path, apparently frightened by some unseen enemy. Then the squirrel swung around a sharp bend in the trail and was lost from sight.

Murdox growled as the squirrel carried him away from his companions. Quickly the path narrowed again, funneling into a narrow lane. In the next instant, the squirrel came to a dead stop. Murdox decided that it wasn't fear that stopped the creature. Apparently its short little legs could no longer carry it forward. When it realized that running was no longer an option, it just stopped. That was the same terrifying moment it came to the simple conclusion that it was slowly sinking into the ground.

Murdox wasn't really sure if it was the sudden stop or the wild thrashing and flailing in the quicksand that caused him to be hurtled from his seat, but either way he was suddenly airborne. Murdox flipped head over heels in the air, completely out of control. Everything was rolling over in slow motion. Ground, sky, ground, sky--this wasn't going to end well.

He was actually pleasantly surprised when he only made a loud squishing sound on impact. Granted, he had landed on his backside, but he wasn't in any particular pain considering the circumstances. When he tried to flip himself over he realized that he, too, was swiftly sinking.

By that time Kase and Asher had caught up with the fleeing squirrel. Asher quickly tied a line of rope around his waist and handed the other end to Kase, who wound it around a tree. Asher waded cautiously into the sand pit and was able to reach the squirrel before it had sunk too deep. He was then able to lead the spooked animal gently out of the shallow quicksand and onto firm ground.

Murdox wasn't so lucky, though. He was too deep in quicksand to be reached and was rapidly sinking ever-deeper into the bog. Asher untied the rope and tossed it to Murdox, who was now nearly up to his head in muck. Murdox snapped at the rope with his jaws but simply couldn't reach it. He was sinking deeper and deeper. Asher hauled in the rope and tried again. By now only Murdox's snout was visible, sticking out of the sand.

The next throw was perfect. The thin line landed directly in the open maw of the trapped wolf-dog. Murdox grabbed the rope with his teeth and with Kase's help, Asher dragged him from the pit.

When Murdox finally got his feet on firm ground, he tried to shake out his coat. In a wave of motion, the wolf-dog shook the quicksand from his fur. The shaking started at his head and spiraled down to his tail. He managed to cover both Kase and Asher with wet sand, but neither seemed to care--they were just glad their companion was safe.

The quicksand pit was huge. It took them nearly an hour to circumvent the soggy snare. When they finally found a spot to cross, it required wading through muddy waters up to their waists, but the squirrels refused to be ridden. In the end, Asher was forced to lead the animals one at a time to the opposite side. Once they were finally back on firm ground, they managed to regain the path out of the swamp... but they were far from being out of trouble. The trail that led them around the quicksand had also pointed them in the direction of another lethal denizen of the swamp.

They came upon yet another split in the road and had to make a decision. It was starting to get late in the day, and all of them were hungry--especially Murdox.

Kase looked down each of the two paths. "The one to the left seems to be the more well-beaten path. The one to the right appears less traveled.... Now where have I heard that before?"

Murdox's stomach was growling, and he ignored the boy. "Let's just take the more beaten path... not because I have any sixth sense about this or anything, but I really don't want to spend the rest of the afternoon trying to make a decision."

Kase and Asher look at each other and shrugged. By mutual agreement, they all set off on the more travelled path.

They had been following it for some time when they first noticed the smell.

Kase scrunched his nose. "This place stinks."

Asher and Murdox had caught a whiff of the stench early on but had been hoping that something had simply crawled off the side of the path and died nearby.

When Kase spoke up, they realized the smell had been getting worse.

Asher decided he had better start watching the trees more closely, and he didn't like what his keen eyes soon saw. "Let's turn around," he advised.

Kase and Murdox looked at the ranger in surprise.

"Why?" Kase glanced around at the trees. "Sure, it stinks, but we can't afford to waste any more time."

Then he noticed the look in the ranger's eye and decided to listen to his advice.

It was too late. Sneaking up behind them were two of the biggest crocodiles Kase had ever seen. The not-so-funny thing about them was that they each had six legs… not to mention what looked like a thousand teeth.

Asher then spotted four more of them between the trees. "Come on, let's get out of here!" he called.

The squirrels leapt down the path with the three companions holding on with all their might. The path was covered in a thin layer of water and quickly getting muddy. The squirrels pounded through the filthy water, but it was getting deeper, deep enough to prevent them from seeing what was ahead of them. In an instant, the bottom fell out from under them and took even the animals by surprise.

They had fallen into a deep, murky pool of rancid water. To Kase's and Murdox's relief, squirrels could swim, albeit not very well. To help the struggling animals, the companions climbed off their saddles and started swimming for themselves.

This wasn't a trap they had stumbled into--this was a crocodile's nest. The crocodiles had now taken up chase and were moving exceedingly fast on their six legs.

Asher reached the other side of the black pool first, followed by Kase, then Murdox. Kase pulled his pack from his back and was digging into it while they waited impatiently for the squirrels to arrive. Thinking quickly, Asher had grabbed his bow when he dismounted from his squirrel. He stood at the water's edge, taking aim at the approaching crocodiles.

Kase held the elf's arm to stop him from firing and then brandished a metal container about the size of a soda can. Warnings and instructions were stenciled in big black letters across its yellow label under the title *SLEEPING GAS*.

Kase looked a little guilty. "I… procured this from the armory the other night. Thought it might come in handy."

He handed it to Asher, who pulled the small pin from the cartridge and hurled it across the pool. It landed in the middle of the enraged crocodiles and immediately began spewing forth a yellow gas. By then the squirrels had finally reached the group and were slogging out of the water.

Kase watched the yellow fog spread out over the water hole. "That won't kill them, just put them out for a while."

Asher was pleased that he didn't have to shoot the crocodiles. He didn't blame them. He would have protected his home in the same manner if trespassers came trampling in. Without hesitation, the party remounted their squirrels and began following the path again. They were all physically exhausted, and they dearly hoped they would make it out of this treacherous swamp alive.

Eventually the path became more and more passable. The weather was clearing, and they managed to feel hope once again. It had taken them the rest of the day and well into the evening to escape, but now they could finally see the stars gleaming in the night sky. Traversing the swamp had not been easy, but they had finally made it out.

When Asher decided it was safe, they found a small clearing and made camp. They were bruised, bleeding, and covered from head to toe in foul-smelling mud. It was time to get some much-needed rest.

Exhausted by the day's trials, the little company made camp under a moonlit sky within the valley of a narrow ravine. Surrounded by fragrant pine trees, they built a roaring fire and prepared an evening meal. Asher put together a stew of dried meat and vegetables. It wasn't exactly gourmet fare, but the members of the small party cleaned their plates without a single word.

The moon was high in the sky when they finally washed and dressed their wounds as best they could. Totally worn out, they crawled off silently to get some well-deserved rest. With food in their stomachs, and aching muscles finally relaxed, it took only a few moments for each of them to drift into a deep sleep.

-Chapter Six-
The Ocean of Sand

As dawn cast a warm glow on the new morning, Kase awoke slowly and removed the hood that had kept him warm during the night. Rubbing his dry eyes, he watched Murdox pad off silently into the pine forest and listened to Asher stirring the burnt embers of the previous evening's fire. He got up and walked painfully over to Asher, who was preparing a light breakfast.

Asher glanced at the boy and then poured him a warm cup of tea. "This should help your sore muscles."

Kase accepted the tea with a groan. "So, what does today hold in store for us?"

Asher looked up from his pots and pans. "Well, first of all, we'll cross over some light hill country to reach the Ocean of Sand. By my best guess, we should be seaside by early afternoon."

Kase wondered what an ocean of sand might be like.

Murdox had slipped quietly back into camp. "Did someone say breakfast? Why, yes, I most certainly would like something to eat."

"Oh, stuff it, you overfed varmint. We'll eat soon enough."

With his head tilted at an angle, Murdox looked up at the boy. "Okay, I'll tell you what you want to know, simply because I want to hurry up and eat."

Kase tried to appear confused. "Tell me what?" Then he decided that playing dumb just wasn't worth it. "Well... you know I'm going to ask anyway, so go ahead and tell me. What exactly is an ocean of sand?"

Murdox shook his head and grinned. "I thought as much…. Actually, the Ocean of Sand is quite a mystery. It's not really liquid, nor is it actually sand, but more like something in between. And it stretches farther than the eye can see."

Kasc remembered yesterday's ordeal in the swamp quite vividly. "Like quicksand?"

Murdox nodded. "Yeah, kind of, but more like a sand milkshake… extra thick. Unlike quicksand, though, you can actually swim in the stuff. Honestly, you'll just have to see it to believe it."

Asher added, "We should be able to find a port near the coast. There, we'll have to hire a ship to sail us across the expanse."

Kase decided not to ask any more questions. It was going to be another long day, and they needed to use the time here to eat a quick meal and pack for the journey ahead.

Passage through the hill country was, for the most part, uneventful. Riding squirrel-back garnered them some strange looks as they traveled through smaller villages on the way to the coast, but no real trouble assailed them. Murdox did his best to keep his mouth shut and tried not to stir up trouble with the locals. Just after noontime, pretty much as Asher had surmised, they rose to the top of a grassy knoll and the ocean came into view.

Kase eyed the Ocean of Sand. "Cool! It looks just like one of those art projects we used to make in school. You know, the ones with the different colored sand in the funny-shaped bottles."

Asher and Murdox had no idea what he was talking about, but they nodded politely in agreement.

Outward from the coast, the sea changed color; from a light turquoise blue near the beach to a deep cobalt blue farther out to sea. Small ocean waves lapped quietly onto the shore in gentle sets. Kase spotted a few ships sailing along the coast, pitching and rolling in the light offshore waves.

The boy pointed down the beach. "Look down the coast. There's a small harbor and what looks like a seaport. Just off the pier, there, it looks like those might be warehouses."

Asher had also seen the buildings and turned his squirrel in their direction. "Come on... let's not dally." He trotted down the hill toward the harbor.

Kase followed behind. "Hopefully, we're in luck, and that's a shipping port."

Murdox took up the rear. "I guess it looks as good as any."

As they approached the town, it became apparent that some kind of festival was under full steam. Banners and pennants flew in a dizzying array of colors. Kase could feel the ground rumbling with excitement. All types of creatures, big and small, danced in the streets, laughing and stumbling in time with the music that filled the air. The company dismounted their squirrels and hitched them to a post near the city gates.

Kase was excited. "Let's have a look!"

Just as they passed through the gate to the city, a band of drunken dwarves intercepted a group of gnomes and started dancing arm in arm with them. The disorderly collection took one look at Murdox and quickly pulled him into their ranks.

The little fellows decided that a song was in

order and proceeded to dance and hum a little tune in the wolf-dog's ear. The group was hopping and skipping to the sounds of the festival. Murdox couldn't for the life of him break free from the little guys.

Somehow, in his struggle to escape, Murdox managed to end up face down in a puddle of mud, surrounded by filthy, wet little men who couldn't help but splash in the dirty water. Unable to hold back their laughter, Kase and Asher pulled him from the puddle just as he tried to bite into one of the gnomes.

Asher could barely keep a straight face as he tried to be stern. "Stop this nonsense!" he told the small men. Soon he was laughing again, so hard that he could scarcely stand upright. "We have to find a ship. Let's head for the harbor and have a look."

It was painfully clear to Murdox that his companions had gotten a good laugh at his expense. In the way that only a wet dog can, Murdox shook himself dry by spraying muddy water in every direction. Strangely enough, and to his secret satisfaction, neither Kase nor Asher found much humor in this.

The travelers then spoke with nearly a dozen

ships' captains, but they could find no one willing to make an immediate crossing. Most of the ships had already arranged their schedules, and the rest were simply unwilling to leave the festival.

Just as they had decided to give up and try another town farther down the coast, a strange, gnarled old seaman approached them.

"I understand yer looking fer a ship," he said. "I know of one."

Asher looked the man over. "Where?"

"Fer a small token, I'll tell ya," said the ragged old gent, who held out a wrinkled palm.

Kase reached into his pocket and pulled out a piece of gold. "You'll get this if your information is correct, but I'll not hand it over until you have found us the vessel you speak of."

Murdox looked up at Kase with what might actually be called pride, although the wolf-dog would never admit to that.

Fortunately for them, the old seaman was correct, and his information did lead them to a ship. At the far end of the harbor, hidden away in a boathouse with a butcher shop in the front, was a ship for hire. They went into the shop to look for the captain and were given directions to where he could be found. The butcher told them that the captain's name was Sternfoot, and his office was located in the alley directly behind the shop. They went looking for him and found a black door, labeled *Overseas Import and Export.*

Kase knocked, and a middle-aged man in green trousers and a puffy white shirt opened the door.

"Are you Captain Sternfoot?" Kase inquired.

"Who's askin'?"

Kase looked confused. "Well, we are, of course…. We're looking for a ship to sail us across the Ocean of Sand to the shores of Moog. We have money and will pay what you ask. Time is of the essence--we need to leave immediately."

Captain Sternfoot smiled. "If you've got the loot, I'll do as you ask. It just so happens I was headed in that direction this very night."

Previously Asher and Kase divvied up a stack of gold coins the elf queen had given them, and the boy eagerly showed off what he had.

The Captain counted the coins and grinned. "You three have yourselves a ship. Gather your things, and return here in two hours. We leave at six o'clock tonight."

With that, the company quickly returned to their squirrels, who were thankfully still tied up where they had left them. Asher made arrangements with a local farmer to board the animals at his nearby ranch--the Badlands of Moog would be hazardous, rocky terrain, and the squirrels would not be of much use to them in that type of country. Asher explained to the farmer that if they didn't return within a few days, another elf would be along to collect them. He later explained to Kase that he had made previous arrangements with an elven scout in Greylok. The scout was to travel to the shores of the Ocean of Sand and be on the lookout for the three squirrels. He was also to report back with any news of the company's fate if they had not returned by that time.

Six o'clock came, and the three travelers headed for the ship. They spotted it immediately, tied to the end of the pier not far from the butcher shop. It was fashioned of dark teakwood and resembled an old

Spanish galleon. Its interior was furnished lavishly with polished woods and cushy leather sofas. The captain showed them to their individual staterooms and made them feel at home. He would serve an evening meal within the hour, and they were invited to join him at his table. They stowed their gear and explored the rest of the ship before dinner.

Needless to say, Murdox was the first to show for dinner. Shortly thereafter, Kase and Asher joined him. They each took a seat around an old wooden table surrounded by comfortable high-back chairs. Food in large quantity was being served by a couple of the crew. A whole roasted turkey was set in front of the captain, who immediately began tearing off one of the legs.

Unmindful of his mouth, the captain sprayed them with bits of food and spittle as he started to speak. "First off, I'll need to tell ya that the Ocean of Sand is no simple crossing. It's a dangerous and tricky passage, and I'm one of few who ever ventures far from the sight of land. Most of the boats only sail the coastline, shipping their wares from one port to the next. For the most part, it's simply too dangerous to earn a living by crossing this sandy expanse. It takes great daring and a good deal of luck to make it across safely."

Kase allowed his eyes to wander about the salon when he noticed for the first time that the crewmembers serving the meal were wearing weapons. When the boy tried to get a better look the crewman caught his eye, and with a sly grin, showed off a mouthful rotting teeth. Something now seemed a bit odd about the warm invitation for dinner, and the lavish rooms they were given. He made a mental note to ask the captain a few questions, and pay better attention to its crew.

The captain continued his story. "We'd best keep an eye out for rogue sand storms that could toss this ship into little pieces... and I shan't forget the formidable sand serpents that prowl these oceans for unsuspecting vessels. But don't ya worry. I've sailed this ocean a hundred times, and aside from an incident with a rogue dune wave, I've encountered very little trouble."

Kase couldn't put his finger on it exactly, but he was a bit troubled by the captain. "So, Captain, what's up with the cannons and the harpoon gun mounted on the forward deck?"

Sternfoot looked the boy square in the eye. "Ahhh, they be just for show. Helps bring in the traveling customers, ya know."

Kase was a bit skeptical about this but kept further comments to himself.

Later that evening, well after they all had gone to bed, Kase was awakened by a commotion on deck just outside his cabin. He quietly pulled back his curtain and peeked out the window. It was dark, but he could vaguely see another ship sailing alongside theirs. It appeared to him that a sailor on their ship was standing behind the harpoon gun, which was now facing the other ship in threat. Another was raising a black flag with a white skull and crossbones emblazoned on it, while the crew tossed heavy grappling hooks efficiently at the other vessel.

A glowing moon slipped out from behind a line of clouds, enabling the boy to see better. Under the pale moonlight, he recognized the harpooner to be Captain Sternfoot. He was peering through an ancient metallic sight while making adjustments to the weapon, apparently targeting the other craft. He twisted knobs and flipped switches until he seemed satisfied with what he saw.

The captain then slowly pulled back the trigger and fired the weapon at the other ship. With hardly a sound, the harpoon gun released a long, barbed, metallic shaft from its barrel. It sailed through the air pulling behind it a line of rope that was still attached to the gun. In an instant the harpoon crashed into the hull of the other boat.

The crew pulled hard on the rope and dragged the other ship alongside their own. A plank of sorts was fashioned between the two boats, and the lines were tied off. Weapons were handed out to the crewmen, who immediately began boarding the other vessel and offloading cargo efficiently from the other ship onto theirs.

Kase then heard Captain Sternfoot quarreling with a dignified-looking officer who he presumed was the captain of the other ship. To Kase's horror, Captain Sternfoot pulled out a devilish-looking curved blade and brandished it against the neck of the other man. Kase could barely hear the conversation, but he most certainly understood what Captain Sternfoot wanted.

Sternfoot held the knife to the man's throat. "We're going to offload your cargo. Don't cause any problems and nobody gets hurt. You just remember that the dread pirate Sternfoot let you live this night."

That was more than enough for Kase. Quietly as a mouse, he got up from his bed and tiptoed cautiously into Murdox's room. The wolf-dog was sleeping soundly with his feet in the air, snoring up a storm. His legs were beating back and forth in the air as if he were running from something. From past experience Kase knew better than to wake Murdox from his sleep--but this was worth it.

He gently nudged Murdox on the shoulder, very carefully avoiding his teeth for fear of losing a hand. "Wake up, you fur ball!"

Murdox awoke with a start and flipped to his side. He looked up at Kase and finally realized where he was.

"What do you want? I was dreaming of... well, you don't need to know."

Kase explained, "We're on a pirate ship. Captain

Sternfoot is actually 'the dread pirate Sternfoot.' Right now he's robbing another ship that's tied up alongside ours. He's got a big, curved knife, a Jolly Roger flag is flying, and that harpoon gun on the deck is most certainly not for show."

Murdox was shaking his head, trying to wake himself up more fully. "Well, that definitely has me interested. Are sure you weren't just dreaming all this? You did eat a good bit of chili, you know."

Kase started to get upset. "Just stop second-guessing me, and have a look for yourself."

Murdox was still half asleep and rolled back over onto his other side. Kase tried to wake him again, but Murdox would have none of it.

Finally Kase gave up and went looking for Asher. He found him sound asleep in his quarters. Kase noted that Asher's quarters were a level below his own and under the waterline, or in this case sand-line, of the boat. There was no way he could have heard any commotion at all. Kase tried his best to enter the room quietly, so as not to startle the elf. Before Kase even had a chance to nudge him awake, Asher was up and staring right at him.

A bit startled by the reaction, Kase quickly explained the entire scenario to Asher, who listened intently. Without any argument, the two of them sneaked quietly back to Kase's room.

When they finally got there, Kase pulled back the curtain and peered into the night. They looked everywhere but couldn't find anything out of the ordinary. The harpoon gun was facing forward and lashed to the deck as before. There was no skull, no crossbones… nothing. To make matters worse, a heavy fog had rolled in within the past few minutes, obscuring their vision. The fog was so thick that even if a ship were right next to them, they probably wouldn't be able to see it anyway. From what they could see, nothing out of the ordinary was in sight. They were simply sailing smoothly along on a black, foggy sea at night.

Asher looked patiently at Kase. "It was the chili. It always does the same thing to me. Just go back to sleep, and think happy thoughts." Then he crept silently back to his room.

"But… but… I know what I saw," said Kase to

no one, "and I didn't eat the chili."

Kase crept onto the deck and searched from stem to stern but could find no proof of what he'd seen earlier. At the back of the boat, he found a couple of the crew playing a late-night game of cards. He asked them if they had seen or heard anything strange that evening, but they just looked at him blankly and refused to reveal anything out of the ordinary.

Kase put on a confused expression. "Oh, well… I thought I heard something. I must just have been dreaming it."

They bid him good evening and resumed their game. He was finally starting to believe it really was just a dream. He made his way to his room and fell asleep again, a good bit perplexed but without much difficulty.

By morning the Sand Sea had turned rough. Its beautiful blue color had changed to a dark foreboding green. Heavy waves rolled the ship from side to side. The sky was gray and menacing. Fiery red streaks of lightning blasted the ocean with thunderous claps.

Captain Sternfoot was on deck, yelling at his crew. "Batten down the hatches, stow the mizzen mast, and get this ship ready for a rough one!"

Kase, Asher, and a very green-looking Murdox came onto deck to see if there was anything they could do. The captain ordered them below deck to help tie down anything that might roll around. Suddenly a thunderous blast crackled just outside the window, and electric fire struck the ocean a few hundred feet from the ship. Sand billowed more than a hundred feet into the air, leaving in its wake a huge, hollow crater that slowly began to refill itself with the flowing sand.

The company needed little coaxing to help out in the cabin below. Murdox was the first to go as he staggered below deck. Asher and Kase followed shortly after. Within an hour, the seas became wild. The ship beat into the wind, tossing it headlong into gigantic waves of sand. Thunder blasted their eardrums as the air sizzled from red-hot lightning.

Waves of sand crashed into the hull of the boat. The bow of the ship plowed through one massive wave after another, spraying tons of the strange, sandy substance across the open deck. The ship was tossed from side to side in an agonizing, deathly dance.

Everyone onboard huddled below deck, hanging onto anything that was bolted down.

Anything that wasn't tied down became a flying health hazard. A barrage of wine bottles broke free from their racks and hurtled at Asher, but he ducked out of their way just in time.

"Watch out!" he yelled and barely caught one of the bottles in mid flight--an instant before it could crash into Murdox's head. The wolf-dog looked up but was far too weak from his bout of seasickness to even thank him.

Captain Sternfoot had lashed himself to the wheel on deck. He steered the ship valiantly through the immense waves. Sand and debris assaulted him, relentlessly blasting him in the face. Without fail he held on to the great wooden steering wheel and maneuvered the boat across the waves.

The boat traveled up and over wave after wave. The sea was giving its all to sink the tiny vessel, but the captain held tightly to the wheel, not for a second giving in to the violent ocean. Time and time again, crisscrossing waves nearly brought the boat to the point of capsizing. In every instance he managed to right the vessel at the last moment and prevent a disaster.

Eventually the seas began to ease, and the crew was able to return to the deck. With their help the boat was gradually stabilized. The waves were now diminishing in size, and they could resume a more controlled course.

By early afternoon the seas finally settled down. The sky began to clear, and the sun peeked through the clouds. Kase and Asher were on deck helping to clean up while Murdox recovered from his seasickness. Captain Sternfoot directed the crew to repair the damage and ordered that the sails be unfurled.

"Sand spout at one o'clock!" yelled a lookout who was stationed high in the crow's nest on top of the mast.

A blue tornado was moving rapidly in their direction. Most of the storm had already passed, and Kase couldn't determine the source of the tornado. Somehow the sand spout seemed to be coming right toward them.

The captain shouted out orders. "It's a Sand

Serpent! Man the guns!"

The captain and one of the crewmen manned the harpoon gun while his first mate took over command of the helm. The crewmen inserted a vicious-looking barbed shaft into the gun, and Sternfoot aimed the weapon at the blue tornado. The rest of the men stationed themselves at each of the cannons, loading them with artillery rounds.

Kase made a mental note that this looked like an awfully familiar sight. He frowned to himself, thinking *'Just for show,' my behind!*

The blue tornado spun right at them, but just as it was about to ram the ship, it suddenly veered off and began circling the vessel. Fine, powdery sand sprayed over the ship and its crew. The tornado went round and round the boat, seeming to be in complete control of its motions. Without warning, a glittering blue head with gold-tinged scales and red eyes emerged from the center of the maelstrom.

Circling the ship, the serpent examined the vessel thoroughly with the aid of its long, sinuous neck. The creature eyed each of the crew and gave the ship a big sniff with two damp, sandy nostrils. Then it dove back into the ocean and surfaced directly in front of the vessel as the swirling tornado of sand died away and fell back into the sea.

The beast held out two giant fins and thrust them into the bow of the ship. Everyone on the vessel who wasn't holding onto something was thrown forward from the sudden halt. When the ship came to rest, the serpent dove back into the ocean and coiled its snake-like body around the vessel. Then the head of the beast emerged without warning on the other side of the vessel, its golden scales sparkling in the afternoon sun. The sand serpent now stared directly at the captain with fierce, glowing, red eyes and bared a toothy grin. It continued to smile with a venomous smirk as it spoke.

"Well, well… I think I've found myself a thief. I thought we had an arrangement here. I promised that I would leave your vessel unscathed and allow you to go about your business of plundering the shipping lanes. In return for my kindness, I would collect a bounty of that oh, so tasty cargo of yours."

The captain looked hurt. "Well, yes, we did… I

mean, we do have a fine business arrangement going on, but I haven't seen you in weeks. The other ships are starting to think we've gone soft or simply given up the trade."

The captain tried his best to remain calm and controlled under the circumstances. "Just last night I had to commandeer a vessel without your help. How exactly do you expect me to run a pirate operation if the muscle hasn't been here to harass the other ships? I even heard a few rumors that you were seen floating belly up, that you'd bought the farm, as they say."

Kase decided that the serpent didn't look quite so big anymore. He had let his giant head droop forward and seemed to be pouting. The creature sank a bit deeper into the sand, looking like a whimpering schoolboy after being given a good scolding.

The dejected serpent whined, "I suppose you're right… I haven't been feeling like myself as of late. I'm just not in the mood to create mayhem on the open seas anymore. I've been seeing a therapist, you know. My doctor thinks it's some kind of mid-life crisis."

Captain Sternfoot looked up at the big creature

and nodded his head. Then he turned to his crew and ordered a few crates of last night's booty to be brought on deck.

Taking pity on the creature, the captain said, "We'll just let this one slip by. How about you have yourself a nice meal, and we'll call it even?"

The crew showed up on deck, burdened with three enormous crates. One of the crewmen opened the boxes with a crowbar and displayed its contents to the drooling sand serpent.

The aroma of sausages, bratwurst, and frankfurters filled the air. Murdox nearly passed out with delight. All thoughts of the earlier bout of seasickness completely fled his mind, but the sand serpent had his own plans for the bounty and stuffed his head into the treasure-trove of fatty meats, eating to his heart's delight.

Kase whispered into Murdox's ear. "I'll bet this is why it costs so much to get a hot dog at a ball game these days. Sternfoot has control of the shipping lanes! He uses the sand serpent to scare away the other ships. He's hard-nosing the competition out of the picture. He can then command an inflated price for his booty. I'm sure he has some kind of deal with the meat packagers, too. They probably look the other way when he arrives with shipload after shipload of meat."

Murdox was listening but could hardly take his eyes from the crates of food.

The serpent finished his snack and tried unsuccessfully to remove a frankfurter that had gotten wedged between his teeth. He picked at his fangs while pondering what to say. "All right, this is what I'll do. Once every month I'll rough up a ship at random. Then I'll let them know it comes with compliments of the dread pirate Sternfoot… and just because I'm such a nice guy, I'll even throw in a casual one now and again. I'll toss the boats from side to side and give them a good shakedown. That should keep them plenty nervous."

Captain Sternfoot smiled. "Excellent arrangement! I am pleased to continue doing business with you."

With that, the snake-like sand serpent smiled his toothy smile and dove headfirst back into the ocean without another word.

Captain Sternfoot turned his attention to the

three companions, but Murdox had somehow slipped by and managed to get his head into one of the crates of meat.

The captain looked at Kase and Asher squarely in the eye and said, "I suppose I'm just going to have to kill you now."

Murdox dropped a half-eaten brat and lifted his head from the crate. Without warning, several of the crewmen produced long, curved swords from their belts, while the rest drew strange-looking pistol-like weapons. The crew quickly began to circle around the companions before they could react.

Asher looked over at Kase and Murdox. He nodded, knowing exactly what the others were thinking. Asher moved like the wind and slammed headfirst into the pirate closest to him. Murdox leapt in a single bound and took a big bite out of another of the treacherous crewmen.

In the confusion, Kase made a dash below deck to retrieve his backpack from his cabin. A fat pirate with a red bandanna around his head chased after him. Kase ran for his life down the narrow passageways, tossing anything that wasn't tied down at his pursuer. He finally gained enough distance on the pirate to lose sight of him, made it to his room, and managed to sling the pack onto his back.

The fat pirate caught up and began searching the rooms. Kase was barely a step ahead of him and could think of nothing better to do than hide behind the door of his cabin. Fortunately for him, this was a well-built ship, and his door was made of solid mahogany wood. When the pirate stuck his fat head into the room in search of him, Kase slammed the door right into his face with all his might. The dazed and bleeding pirate staggered back a few steps and slumped against the far wall of the corridor.

Kase shot out of the room like a bullet and ran down the stairs to recover Asher's pack from his cabin. All the crewmen were occupied on deck, and no further trouble beleaguered the boy. When he had retrieved everything he could, he bolted back up to the deck of the ship to help his friends.

Asher had managed to find himself a sword. He looked like a regular swashbuckler, easily holding off three of the pirates. Swords were slashing in every direction, clinking and clattering in a frenzied commotion. One of the pirates fired off a round from his pistol, but Asher was able to dodge the shot miraculously. When another one of the men fired off a shot. Asher instantly pulled away from the battle and deflected the bullet with the sword. A notch was ripped from the weapon, and the projectile slammed harmlessly into one of the wooden walls alongside the ranger. Without losing a moment of concentration, he renewed his fight and advanced on the other sword-bearing pirates.

The captain and four of his cronies had cornered Murdox. The wolf-dog was hunkered down low, exposing all his teeth and growling up a storm. His display allowed Kase enough time to sneak up behind the captain and kick him in the back of the knee. This gave Murdox the opportunity he needed. The big wolf-dog plowed into the other three pirates, knocking them to the ground.

Murdox and Kase then ran in Asher's direction, who was now holding off four of the pirates single-handed. He was slashing away with his sword and deflecting bullets at the same time. The hale of gunfire was quickly whittling away the metal of his blade.

Realizing this, one of the pirates took careful aim and blasted away the remainder of the weapon. Asher then tossed the nub of the sword at the closest pirate and scampered up the mainsail mast. A few of the pirates followed, but he managed to kick them out of the way on his ascent.

Kase and Murdox continued to distract the pursuing pirates and kept them preoccupied while Asher made his move. Murdox hesitated for just a moment and allowed a particularly fat, nasty buccaneer to catch up to him. When the pirate thought he was about to tackle the wolf-dog, Murdox ducked out of the way at the last second. The pirate slammed to the deck, and Kase knocked him over the head with an oar.

Asher was now at the top of the mast, waiting for Kase and Murdox to lure the rest of the pursuing pirates to the center of the ship. They both had a pretty good idea of what he was up to. Asher withdrew a wicked-looking blade from his belt and slashed a big chunk out of the sail. He then grabbed hold of the exposed material and leapt off the wooden brace he had been standing on. He came flying down from high above the ship, tearing the sail away from the mast to slow his fall as he hurtled to the wooden floor. He hit the deck with a perfectly executed tumble, still holding onto the end of the sail. What was left of the sail now covered most of the crew.

Kase and Murdox had figured out exactly what Asher was doing, and just in time, were able to position themselves out of harm's way. Asher held onto the sail and ran straight into the mass of pirates. With sail still in hand, he ducked down low and was able to sweep the feet out from under the confused group. In an instant he had managed to entangle them in the canvas and allow time for an escape.

Kase yelled to Asher, "What now?"

Asher shrugged and pointed to the front of the ship. "Now we jump!"

Murdox's eyes grew wide with fear. "That's the plan?"

Kase tossed Asher his pack, and the three of them made a dash for the bow of the ship. They stopped at the railing, looked back in the direction of the ensnared pirates, and in unison leapt over the side, right into the Ocean of Sand.

Before long the pirates were able to cut themselves free of the sail and follow them to the edge of the ship. The pirates headed to the ship's railing, but not into the sandy sea below.

Captain Sternfoot limped over to the side of the vessel and leaned into the railing with all his weight. "I would do the merciful thing and blast you with my cannons, but after that little incident, I think we'll leave you three to the denizens of the deep. I read somewhere that if you get swallowed by one of the serpents, it actually takes weeks for you to die while it slowly digests you." The Captain looked at the mess Asher had made of the sail. "Pity, though--I would have enjoyed killing you myself. Do you have any idea how much a sail costs?" He turned his back and started shouting orders to his men.

The three allies treaded sand and watched as the ship sailed off into the distance.

Kase looked at his friends with a smirk. "See, I

told you they were pirates. Maybe you'll listen to me next time."

Irritated, Murdox and Asher glared back at him as they waited for the ship to sail out of sight.

Kase flipped open his magical backpack, doing his best to keep the sand from spilling into it, and withdrew a deflated life raft. "I had hoped it wouldn't come to this," he said as he pulled on the red handle attached to the raft.

Whoosh! A big yellow raft inflated in front of their eyes. "I always wondered why Dad always stuck this in here, but now I'm sure glad I kept it."

They climbed into the rubber raft and pulled free two plastic paddles that were strapped to the side. Kase and Asher dipped the paddles into the sandy ocean and started rowing in the direction of Moog.

Asher was massaging a growing bruise on his arm. "I don't much care for paddling, but the alternative would have been considerably worse. I'm glad that you had the sense to retrieve that magic pack of yours from your cabin."

The sun was just starting to set on a pretty bad

day when an unexpected voice thundered from behind them.

"Feeling kinda guilty about this whole mess."

Kase, Asher, and Murdox slowly turned their heads to the back of the raft and found themselves looking right into the mouth of the sand serpent who had perpetrated the whole disaster. Turquoise blue sand cascaded from the serpent's lower jaw and onto Murdox's head as he spoke, scaring the wolf-dog half to death.

"Take it easy. I'm not going to bite...." The serpent then bent down low and gave Murdox a quick sniff. "...even though you do smell a lot like bratwurst." He straightened up again. "The name is Shaley O'Rielly. I thought you guys were part of his crew. How was I supposed to know you were the customers?"

The serpent undulated its body to stay afloat in the sandy sea, causing their small craft to rock back and forth. "I had no idea that the old captain was actually hurting people," he continued. "When I saw what he did to you... well, let's just say that was the last straw. Our arrangement was to rough up the boats a bit, but never did this deal involve actually hurting anyone. Heck, humans taste rotten anyway--mostly skin and bones."

The serpent shook its massive head, dumping more sand onto Murdox. "Captain Sternfoot has gone too far this time. I really like those little sausages, but I'm not going to jettison my sense of moral decency for them. Anyway, I digress. How about I give you all a tow to shore?"

Murdox tried to shake the sand from his coat and looked over at Kase.

The boy nodded and then pulled a length of rope from his backpack. "Why not?"

Asher took the rope and fastened it around the creature's neck, then tied the other end to the front of the raft.

Before they knew it, they were skimming along the surface of the sand, leaving a hefty wake behind them. The serpent glided effortlessly in and out of the waves with the little raft secured tightly to its neck. Before they knew it, Shaley O'Rielly had towed them to within sight of land.

The serpent smiled a toothy grin. "This will have

to do ya. I daren't go any farther… wouldn't want to ruin a perfectly bad reputation."

Asher pulled the rope from the creature's long neck and stowed it back in Kase's pack. They thanked the serpent just as dove back into the sand. Hardly a moment later, it resurfaced just behind the raft. "Don't you worry about a thing. As for the dread pirate Sternfoot, I think I shall be tossing his ship before long."

Then the serpent bid them farewell and slipped back beneath the sand.

# -Chapter Seven-
Moog

The land of Moog, for the most part, was a dreary and decidedly unfriendly place, and the cold, damp air didn't improve the company's first impression. A heavy fog had rolled in from the Ocean of Sand and hung low to the ground, chiling all of them to the bone.

The little company rowed into a rocky cove and

beached the rubber raft on the shore. After finding a safe spot to make camp, Asher hastily built a small fire near the entrance of a wind-washed sea cave.

Kase dropped his pack next to the fire and searched through their supplies. He came up with enough food to provide each of them with a light meal.

Asher looked over what they had in stock. "We'll have to ration our supplies, but what we've got should suffice for the next few days."

Murdox groaned but agreed that rationing was their only option.

An hour or so later, with food in their stomachs, they each found a relatively dry spot at the back of the cave and curled up for the evening.

* * * *

The next morning was a bit warmer, but the place was just as bleak as the night before. Asher withdrew Enob's ancient map and studied the old drawings. He looked at the map and made an educated guess as to where they were.

"If my estimation is correct, we should be able to head inland from this location and reach the Dragon's Spine within a day or so. All that's left then is to locate the mountain where the dragon's cave is hidden."

He looked up at them and shook his head. "Don't misunderstand me… we still have a long way to go. This is dangerous country, and we'll be exposed to harsh weather and extremely rocky terrain. Moog is a wild place, and we'll have to be vigilant for predators prowling for an easy meal."

A howl in the distance caught everyone's attention. Fortunately for them, it was too far away to be a threat, so Asher continued with his description of the countryside. "There are only a handful of civilized towns in this country, and they're mostly located along the coast. The creatures that roam these wastelands are big and vicious. This is dragon and raptor country--they rule the sky here--but I've dealt with them before, and I know how to avoid becoming lunch. The leonine are another story, though. We're going to have to keep a watchful eye out for them."

Asher let Kase and Murdox absorb what he said,

but Kase had that all-too-familiar look in his eye.

Murdox saw the look. "Get it over with. Ask your question…," he insisted. Then he decided not to wait for Kase to reply and instead turned to Asher. "Okay…. What are the leonine?"

What he told them was an ancient tale of a long-forgotten war. "Many millennia ago, the Ancient Wars laid waste to the lands. The dark wizards of that time controlled vast stores of power and brought the planet to the brink of destruction. Vile, devastating magic was used to oppress and ultimately bring down the various races of the world.

"Masters of evil magic, greater than anything the world had ever seen, sought to control the lands. The good people of that forgotten age fought back with great might but were easily swayed and brought down by the masters of the dark magic. Eventually, as do all things, time and war balanced out. The evil that had weighed so heavily on the world slowly began to lose its influence over man… but it was too late, for the dark magic that was brought about to fight the wars had gone unchecked and swept across the planet. All the lands became wild and untamed."

Kase and Murdox listened in fascination as Asher continued.

"The evil wizards had tried to combine and mold their individual forces in an attempt to magnify them. This often mutated both man and nature. Many creatures exist today because of such dastardly mutations. Some of them are violent, hateful beings that take pleasure in hunting and killing for sport. The leonine were the first and most dangerous of these.

"Toward the end of the war, the tide of battle was turning toward good. The evil taint began to lose ground. It was the dark wizards' intent to develop a creature that would shift the tide again to evil, once and for all. With that in mind, they created the leonine race from what they deemed were the most useful qualities of man and beast.

"The leonine have the keen physical attributes of a lion--incredible speed and strength and the uncanny senses of a predator. These, combined with man's intelligence and ability to reason, made the creature a formidable foe.

"Fortunately for everyone, the leonine wanted nothing to do with war, nor did they feel any allegiance toward man or wish to follow his orders into battle. They fled and claimed the uncivilized territories in which we are now standing. Now they roam these lands, hunting the local beasts for pleasure and sustenance-- they are creatures that could easily make lunch meat out of us."

Kase and Murdox were staring at Asher with their mouths open. Murdox swiveled his head around, looking for an unseen enemy. "It just goes from bad to worse, doesn't it?" he fumed.

Asher's expression didn't change. "I am afraid it does."

Murdox whimpered. "What do you think, Kase... how's about we get ourselves a nice job driving one of the slugs around town? The pay can't be much worse, and I doubt we'd find ourselves being hunted down too often."

Asher ignored Murdox. "At this time of year, I believe most of the leonine will be farther north. The three-headed abominable snowmen are migrating now, and they are the leonine's favorite food."

Kase visualized lion-men chasing down giant, furry, three-headed snowmen, and he didn't like what he was imagining.

The little group packed their equipment and set off quietly in the early morning light. Trying unsuccessfully to keep dark thoughts from getting the best of them, they headed in the direction of the Dragon's Spine.

By mid-morning, as they topped a windblown hill, they spotted the snow-capped mountains they so desperately sought.

Asher peered into the distance. "If we make good time, we should be in the foothills by nightfall."

Out of nowhere, two imposing shapes suddenly obliterated the sun and cast a strange shadow onto the small company. In an instant, sharp talons seemed to drop from the sky and grab at Kase. A giant, black-winged hawk snatched the boy away from his comrades as he screamed for help. Asher and Murdox had ducked reflexively during the attack and were now helpless to aid Kase in any way.

Asher tried his best to shield Murdox, yelling, "Quick! Make for cover!"

The wolf-dog and the elf ranger ran for a rocky outcropping that might protect them from another aerial assault. Asher dove into his pack and pulled out a long rope. In a flash he quickly climbed to the top of the outcropping and attempted to attract the second of the aerial predators.

Asher was feeling ashamed for not being more careful. He'd been preoccupied with the lay of the land and had simply missed the warning signs. At that moment he made a vow never to let such a thing happen again. He renewed his pledge always to maintain vigilance, especially in places of such extreme danger.

It wasn't difficult to attract the other hawk. The huge bird was circling overhead and had already spotted the two remaining travelers hiding under the ledge. Its penetrating black eyes were fixed on its target. Asher steadied his nerves and made a mental note that this bird was even larger than the one that had captured Kase.

Asher controlled his breathing and slowed his heart rate, anticipating the attack. As the creature pointed its curved beak toward the ranger and lunged straight at him, Asher quickly created a lasso out of the rope. Then the colossal, dark raptor dove headlong toward its prey.

The winged beast kept its eyes fixed on Asher as it began to rotate out of the dive. The hawk then extended its razor-sharp talons in preparation for the strike, but Asher was an instant faster than the beast and leapt into the air just out of its reach.

He was an elf, after all, and an extremely nimble one at that. Elves could perform incredible gymnastic feats on account of their naturally perfect balance, a trait enhanced by millennia of inhabiting the treetops. This was just one of many reasons the elves had taken to living in the Great Forest so harmoniously, entirely unafraid of falling from their aerial homes.

Of course, Asher was more than just an average elf; he was a ranger, and thus trained to challenge the physical limitations of his body. He hurled himself into the air. While still accelerating from his jump, he managed to loop the cord around the hawk's neck. He tugged on the cord to change his direction and then landed on the creature's back.

He pulled hard on the lasso, tightening the loop around the hawk's neck. The bird squawked in protest, tossing itself violently back and forth in the air. Asher held on with all his strength, jamming his thighs into the hawk's sides and pulling on the lasso as hard as he could. The tossing and turning continued, but Asher was determined not to let go. The next few moments were tense, but the big bird finally gave in to the rider and stopped its wild bucking.

Asher found that he could hold on with his knees and steer the hawk with the rope. The bird wasn't keen about this but soon gave in to its rider's demands.

Asher then spotted the hawk that had flown off with Kase and commanded his mount to give chase. He nudged the bird in the sides with his heels and slapped its long neck with one hand. The great hawk was intelligent and understood well enough what the rider was demanding, and it flew hesitantly toward the other bird.

Asher pushed the creature to the limit and quickly closed the distance between the two airborne predators. The hawk carrying Kase soon realized that it was being pursued. The countryside below them had become more rugged and was pocked with long deep fissures and canyons. With Kase firmly held in its talons, the hawk dove low and hugged the ground. It instinctively clutched Kase tighter in its massive claws as it wove and dipped among the rocky spires and windblown outcroppings.

Desperately, Asher pulled hard on the rope and forced his mount to fly downward in a breakneck dive in pursuit of the other bird. The fleeing bird dove low to the ground, dragging the boy across gravel and scraping his legs. Kase screamed bloody murder as the hawk that carried him zigged and zagged in and out of the rocky terrain.

Asher refused to give any ground. He pushed his flying steed onward and continued the deadly chase only inches from the jagged landscape below. Wildly, frantically he flew headlong under stone archways and over razor-sharp outcroppings, through incomprehensible turns and banks, not for an instant giving up his pursuit.

The first hawk held Kase tightly in its claws, pulling him closer to its dark underbelly as it dropped down into a long, deep canyon, barely grazing the edge. It dove for what seemed like an eternity, dipping farther down to a raging river that wound through the center of the canyon.

Asher followed without hesitation, urging his bird onward. Quickly the canyon began to narrow, and it seemed as if the bird's wing tips were grazing the canyon walls. Asher was having difficulty controlling his steed. The narrow walls of the ravine forced his larger bird to fly higher in the canyon, with a scant bit more room for maneuvering.

The gorge turned sharply to the left, then right and left again as the two birds banked sideways, narrowly avoiding collision with the walls. Before Asher could regain his sense of direction, the canyon began to slope sharply downward and suddenly dead-ended in a sheer rock wall. The river cascaded into the drop-off, forming a waterfall that tumbled hundreds of feet into a deep, mist-shrouded sinkhole.

With Kase in hand, the hawk swooped inches

over the falls, nearly drowning the boy in icy, violent spray. The waterfall roared into a black lagoon at the base of the falls. There the river continued into a dark underground cavern.

Asher was unable to control his bird when it spotted the sheer rock face. Instinctively the creature thrust itself upward, clipping the jagged canyon walls as it climbed. Propelled only by sheer momentum, Asher and the creature bounced painfully off the rock face in an uncontrollable upward climb. They reached the upper edge of the cliff and tumbled over its lip.

The second hawk thrust out its long legs and forced itself to run to a halt on the smooth plateau above the canyon. In a cloud of dust, Asher spun the dizzy bird around and, without thinking, ran it back to the edge of the cliff. He forced the creature over the edge and into a dive, straight down toward where Kase and his captor had disappeared. When he spotted the cave, he plunged into its depths without a second thought.

Without realizing it had temporarily lost its pursuer, the smaller hawk had dived headlong into the cavern with its prey grasped tightly in its claws. It zoomed past a viciously sharp-pointed stalactite, banking right, left, up, and over a towering stalagmite that rose from the dark cavern floor. Kase had long since covered his eyes with his hands, no longer able to endure watching their nerve-racking flight.

Panicked, the fleeing bird searched for a way out. With its keen eyes, it quickly spotted light filtering through a crack in the ceiling of the cavern. Guided by instinct, it began a series of tight turns around the various rocky obstacles, making its way toward the light.

The hole in the ceiling was smaller than it had first appeared. The creature was forced to pull in its huge, feathery wings as close to its body as it could, but its bulk was still too much for the narrow opening. It blasted upward through the crack, propelling rocks and dirt in all directions. The creature made it back into daylight, though one of its wings was torn savagely in the escape. A trail of bloodied feathers drifted downward as it climbed into the sky.

Asher was disgusted, thinking that he had lost them in the darkness. He knew the bird must have flown into the cavern, or he would have seen it flying away from the waterfall. He was guiding his bird through a series of narrow rock formations when he spotted the light far above him. It took little coaxing from Asher to pull them into a sharp climb and regain the chase. Attuned to such things, the hawk he was riding had smelled the blood of the other bird.

Excited by the scent, Asher's hawk accelerated its climb and headed straight for the opening. The bird's keen eyes spotted a better exit point in the ceiling, and it sailed out of the cavern without doing itself any harm.

Immediately upon hitting the sunlight, both Asher and his hawk spotted their target. The predator that had so diligently held on to Kase was becoming weary and having trouble keeping itself airborne. Asher saw that one of its wings looked to be injured, and the beast was slowing its ascent.

With the prey still clasped in its talons, the hawk knew that it would have trouble staying aloft. Nonetheless, through some internal drive, it continued to climb ever higher into the sky. Once again it sensed danger and dipped its fierce head to get a look at the pursuers quickly closing the gap.

Then it gauged the weight of its prey and realized that it wasn't going to make it. Reluctantly, it finally released the lunch it had so desperately fought for, and then it wheeled around to limp itself home on the bloodied wing.

Kase was screaming at the top of his lungs. He knew there was nothing he could do to help himself. He recognized clearly that he was going to fall to his death and get splattered across the unforgiving land of Moog. He tried to calm himself and prepare for the inevitable, but all he could manage to do was yell in utter terror.

Asher quickly closed the distance between them. He had seen the hawk release the boy from its claws. He nearly panicked, but the great hawk he was flying knew instinctively what to do and matched speed with the falling prey. Then it reached out cautiously and plucked Kase from the sky with its talons.

Kase was still screaming when he realized that he was no longer falling to his death. Then he heard a familiar voice from above and recognized that it was Asher calling to him.

"How are you down there? Sorry it took so long to find you, but I had to stop along the way for a few errands."

Kase could hardly believe his luck. He was simply shocked that he hadn't been splattered into the ground. "Uh…thanks for saving me!" was about all that came out.

With Kase in tow, Asher turned his great bird around and headed back to where they had left Murdox.

*

The wolf-dog was easy to find. When Asher had leapt from the outcropping into the air, and Murdox had realized what he was attempting, he knew he could do little to help. After the elf had lassoed the second hawk, Murdox had tried his best to follow along below.

In utter amazement Murdox had watched Asher fly off in pursuit of Kase. Not knowing what else to do, he ran along below them, trying to follow the aerial chase. He was a wolf-dog and was fast, but even his quickest pace was not enough to keep up with the hawks.

Murdox tried his best to track them from the ground. Eventually he came to the edge of the canyon and followed the rim as far as he could. Luckily Asher, with his keen elf vision, spotted him from the air.

Asher reined in the giant hawk carefully for a landing, hoping it wouldn't injure Kase in the process. Fortunately the bird understood and let the boy down gently before it landed. Asher brought the bird to a halt and climbed off his back, removing the rope from around his neck. The bird was pleased to be rid of the rope that had bound him but was simply too exhausted to then strike at the elf.

Kase was still dazed and overwhelmed by the ordeal but understood the gravity of the situation and quickly reached into his backpack. He carefully unwrapped a substantial filet of raw steak that he had been saving for Murdox and handed it to Asher.

Asher set down the piece of meat in front of the big bird and warned, "If you don't eat that right now, you're going to have to fight the dog for it."

Meanwhile, a puddle of drool was growing at

Murdox's feet. The hawk took one look at the slavering wolf-dog and quickly snatched up the meat. Then the bird looked back at Asher and in a flutter of black wings, lifted quietly into the air. The three travelers watched until it disappeared into the distance.

Kase was more shaken up from the whole incident than actually hurt. His pant legs had been torn, he was bleeding from a few minor wounds, and his shoulders were sore to the touch, but for the most part he was unharmed. They let him rest a bit while Asher determined their location.

The elf soon remarked that the ordeal had hardly set them back at all. He pointed to the snow-capped peaks in the distance. The fight and flight had actually taken them in the same direction they needed to go.

Murdox looked toward the mountains. "If all goes well from here, and if we can find a ship to return across the Ocean of Sand, do you think we just might make it back in time to save the King?"

Kase was rubbing his swollen shoulders, simply glad to be alive. He looked to Asher for a response.

"We can only hope," the elf replied.

The rest of the day went by without incident. The uneven ground was difficult to traverse, but for the most part the trek wasn't as bad as they feared. Although a few boulders blocked their path, they managed to make fairly good time. By early evening, without any sign of further trouble, they thought they might be in the clear.

They were crossing a field of tall, brown grass with Asher leading the way. "If we can make it just a bit farther to the foothills of the mountains, we'll set up camp there," the ranger told them. "From what I know of the leonine, they tend to avoid the mountains. I'm not exactly sure why they steer clear of high country, but I would venture to guess it's some kind of superstition. In any case, the mountains may provide us a measure of safety from attacks."

They were in the middle of an open savannah of dry grass that had grown so tall that it was mostly over their heads. Asher was trying to see above the stalks. "The foothills into the mountains couldn't be more than a half-mile away," he estimated. "I think we should continue in the direction we're headed."

Kase and Murdox nodded, and the group

continued plodding along. Then Murdox perked up his ears, and Asher became aware of a disturbance in the distance. He grabbed Kase by the hood of his sweatshirt and started dragging him back in the direction from which they had come. The ground beneath them began to rumble and shake violently. Without warning, the grasses around them suddenly exploded with activity. Seemingly out of nowhere came a stampede of men who were striped from head to toe in white and black fur. The men's eyes looked wild and terror-filled, and they were all screaming at the top of their lungs.

Asher quickly tried to determine what to do and where to go. He eyed Kase and Murdox, then threw himself to the ground and covered his head with his arms. The boy and the wolf-dog did the same, just as the wild creatures reached them.

The herd of striped men split down the middle, narrowly avoiding the three companions in their frantic stampede. When the rush had passed, the little company heaved a collective sigh, spitting out dirt and grasses but otherwise unscathed.

Asher remarked, "The zebra men are the

leonines' second favorite food."

All was quiet again for a moment when Murdox suddenly began sniffing the air. Kase and Asher looked around and realized why the zebra men were in such a panic. A small pack of leonine had been chasing their dinner. The travelers froze and tried their best to play dead.

While most of the leonine pack continued after the zebra men, three of the golden-furred leonine halted their chase to investigate the strange-smelling creatures lying in their path. One of the leonine, dressed in nothing more than a loincloth, dropped to all fours. He sniffed each one of the travelers thoroughly while the two other creatures pointed devilishly sharp spears in their direction. The adventurers lay perfectly still.

The leonine were covered from head to toe in light golden fur. Their faces were human but were shaped dramatically like a lion's. They had yellow feline eyes, wet triangular noses, and smiles full of fangs. Their hands and feet resembled elongated paws with sharp, black, curved claws growing from them. Two of them had what Kase would have described as manes that extended from the tops of their heads, around their broad shoulders, and down their chests, and which ended in a point at the center of their bellies.

The leonine who was checking them out had no mane and sported short-cropped hair that came to a point in the middle of her back. She appeared to be female, while the other two were apparently male.

Kase gulped hard, thinking that he now knew why lions were known as the rulers of the jungle.

The female leonine finished smelling them, licked her lips, and made a whining sound to the other two creatures. They responded with a series of growls and hisses. Finally, the biggest of the three thumped his spear on the ground and quieted the other two.

In a blur of motion, the female dropped down and grabbed hold of Kase's ankles. The two males went for Asher and Murdox, but even their feline reflexes weren't fast enough. Asher leapt into the air and gave one of his would-be captors a solid kick to the chest. At the same time, in an amazing flying vault, Murdox opted to go for the throat of the other attacker.

Asher's kick knocked the leonine backwards but

failed to do the damage he was hoping for. With amazing speed and prowess, the leonine recovered himself and spun the blunt end of his spear into the air. In a revolving leap, he flipped himself up and over Asher's head and then with a perfectly executed swing, knocked Asher's legs out from under him.

Asher fell backwards, but although it seemed as if he would crash to the ground, he managed to use his own momentum and flip backwards in a somersault. Without hesitation the leonine made another lunge at the elf. In mid-stride, Asher was able to grab hold of the spear and pull it away from the creature with a rotating motion.

Asher attempted to thump the spear over the leonine's head, but the cat man was too fast and managed to take the blow to the shoulder instead. The leonine quickly rolled out of the way of Asher's next attack and instantly recovered in an offensive posture.

Asher was already exhausted from the day's events and was in no shape to battle with such an impressive fighter. He made the mistake of attempting to jab the creature with the spear by lunging forward. The leonine easily dodged the lunge and while spinning away, was able to wrench the spear from Asher's hand.

With his spear now back in hand, the leonine continued his spin until he was perfectly positioned behind the elf. The leonine swung the spear handle like a baseball bat against the back of Asher's neck. The elf attempted to duck the maneuver but only managed to take the blow to the back of the head. Asher swayed from side to side, and with a thump, fell face-first to the ground.

Murdox was going for the throat of his opponent, but he was caught in midair by the swift, powerful creature, and they both tumbled to the ground. With great effort the leonine flung Murdox off of his chest and leaped into a crouching position.

Murdox rolled away from the toss, hopped to his feet, and dropped his head low. He lifted every hair he could on the back of his neck and pushed back his ears. He narrowed his eyes and curled his upper lip, exposing his own menacing set of teeth. At that point the wolf-dog let loose a guttural growl that would have brought a normal man to tears.

Unfortunately, the leonine was no normal man, and he actually growled right back at the wolf-dog with a loud, roaring rumble. Both of them charged forward and slammed into each other head on. They rolled and tumbled in the tall grass, scratching and biting one another. Both were going for the throat and the eyes, but neither could land a clean shot.

Finally Murdox pulled away from the big cat and attempted to circle around him. He was looking for another way in. He wanted to sink his fangs into the creatures exposed throat. The leonine saw this and baited the wolf-dog. He lifted his head and exposed the unprotected flesh of his throat. Then he extended a clawed hand toward Murdox and curled the fingers repeatedly in the universal come-and-get-me gesture.

Murdox took the bait and made a gravity-defying leap at the leonine. The golden-haired cat managed to catch Murdox in mid flight and catapult the dog head-over-heels into the tall grass. Caught completely unprepared, Murdox flipped through the air and landed far behind the creature. He slammed down hard, head first against the ground, which knocked the wind from his lungs, and he blacked out.

The leonine who was after Kase was in no mood to put up a fight. She decided to trick him instead. She began to lift him by his ankles, and when Kase rolled over and thrashed out of her grip, she backed away. As Kase scrambled to his feet and attempted to block her next move, the cat leapt forward with lightning speed and slammed a roundhouse punch right into him.

Kase just wasn't a warrior.…

* * * *

Kase struggled out of the fog that shrouded his mind as consciousness slowly returned. He was the first to awaken and discover that all three of the travelers were locked in a cage made of hollow, tubular wood that was set into a mud base. He had a headache like no tomorrow and a good bit of dried blood under his nose, and he discovered that he could hardly move his aching jaw. The last thing he could remember was a big, furry fist coming right at him. Thankfully, though, nothing appeared to be broken.

He went to Murdox and Asher to check on their condition. They too were recovering and trying painfully to sit up.

Asher touched the back of his own head gingerly with an injured hand. He almost screamed out in pain but quickly thought better of it.

Murdox's whole body throbbed in agony. Nothing was broken, but he didn't want to think about how stiff and sore he might be by morning.

Asher was checking to see if he had lost any teeth when one of the leonine stopped in front of the cage and looked in on them. The creature found great humor in rattling the cage a bit, but soon lost interest in the trio and wandered off.

Kase was carefully rubbing one of his swollen eyes.

"I guess we're in a bit of a pickle."

Asher looked up. "That we are."

With great effort, Murdox stuck his nose in the air and took a big whiff. "We seem to be alone for the moment. I guess we don't seem worthy enough as opponents for them to post a guard. I can only imagine why we're here, anyway."

Asher looked at the others with a grim smile. "We're going to be breakfast. I would venture to guess some type of stew."

Kase was trying to keep his imagination in check. It was dark, and stars were twinkling in the sky above them. He scanned the area and spotted his and Asher's backpacks lying only a few feet from the cage.

"Let's get our bags and get the heck out of here."

Murdox licked one of his bloodied paws very carefully. "So, how exactly do you plan on making this escape?"

Kase pulled off his shoes and removed the laces. He tied the ends together to make one long lace. Asher realized what Kase was up to and removed his belt buckle. He fashioned a hook out of it and tied it to the end of the shoelace.

Kase took a quick look around to see if the coast was clear and then tossed the hook at his pack. It took a couple of tries, but he managed to snag it and pull it over to the cage. Through the bars, he opened the bag and withdrew the map so Asher could figure out approximately where they were. Kase then began riffling through his things, trying to come up with a decent plan.

By this time it was very early in the morning, maybe three or four hours before dawn, and the moon cast a pale glow over the terrain. With his sharp eyesight, Asher could see the shadowy outline of the mountains just behind them. Luckily for them, the leonine must have camped close to the foothills of the Dragon's Spine. If they could escape, a quick dash to the mountains would hopefully put them out of harm's way… of course, that was if Asher was right, and the leonine wouldn't follow them into the mountains. First they had to get out of the cage.

Eventually Kase withdrew a lock pick and let Asher get to work on the cage door. He then located a miniature chemistry set and placed it on the floor in front of him and Murdox in the moonlight. Kase explained to Murdox what he wanted to do. The wolf-dog smiled at the boy, and they immediately got to work.

Before long they had stirred up a sizzling brew.

Kase pulled a small empty bottle from his pack and poured the concoction into it. The boy then sealed the bottle of their newly created potion and attached a string to the cork. Then he opened another container and poured a powdery substance on the floor to act as a catalyst for their planned surprise.

Asher was working diligently on the cage door. The lock soon snapped open, and Asher returned the lock pick to Kase's pack. Before they left, Kase rigged the bottle to the door of the cage. Then the three prisoners slipped quietly out of the cage and sped into the darkness.

They ran until dawn, until Kase finally fell to his knees, panting. By then they were well into the mountains and were traveling up a narrow canyon that led deep between the jagged peaks above them. Kase collapsed onto a cold, flat rock and tried his best to catch what breath he could.

"I… think… we… got… away."

Asher was looking behind them. "I believe so, but I dare say we shouldn't rest too long. Even if they don't pursue us, we still have precious little time remaining to finish our task and return to the King. Rest for a moment, and then we'll continue."

He resumed his lookout for a few minutes, then turned again to his companions. "What exactly did you two leave for our furry friends back there?"

Kase and Murdox looked at each other and laughed. "We brewed up a batch of super-concentrated red-hot chili powder. Murdox had the bright idea to throw in some catnip for flavoring. The chemicals that will mix together when the cork gets pulled will create a nice little explosion. When they open that door to see where their breakfast has gone… *BOOM!* They're in for a big surprise."

Kase and Murdox laughed some more as Asher smiled broadly.

"Those sensitive noses of theirs won't be right for weeks, and quite frankly I'm not sure what the catnip might do to them. I doubt it will be very pleasant, though."

Asher laughed out loud and said, "I'm fairly certain that if the mountains are not enough to keep them from following us... that most certainly should do the trick."

-Chapter Eight-
Blood Dragon

From what Asher could determine from the map, it looked as though the Blood Dragon's lair should be only a few hours away. They would have to continue following the narrow pass they were in, and eventually they would reach the top of the mountain. From there they would traverse the back side of the great expanse until they came to a winding river.

According to the map, the river flowed into a box canyon that marked the entrance to the dragon's cave.

The travelers had only a brief opportunity to relax. For the moment, there didn't seem to be any sign of pursuit and they rested their weary bones for only as long as they dared. When they felt they could afford to remain there no longer, they pulled themselves together and set off.

The trek was long and hard, and the remainder of the ascent exhausted the already tired trio. After hours of climbing uphill, they finally reached the rim of the mountain. From this high vista they could see the vast range of jagged peaks looming in the distance.

It didn't take Asher long to spot a loose, icy path that led down the back of the mountain, and after another brief rest, they headed toward it. He could see that it disappeared into a narrow ravine, presumably concealing the river they sought.

The small company traveled wearily down the rocky path along the back of the mountain. At this elevation, snow covered the ground and made for difficult travel. It was tough on their knees, but the downhill trek was certainly much easier than climbing up.

Finally by midday they reached a small grove of spruce trees at the entrance to the ravine. There was the river they had sought. The group rested under the boughs, just a few feet from the meandering river, and ate a brief meal in silence.

Asher decided to scout ahead and follow the river into the ravine while Kase and Murdox rested from their ordeal. When he returned from his mission, he took a seat on a fallen log near the others.

"I followed the river for a mile or so into the ravine until it narrowed and flowed right into the side of the mountain. The water forms a shallow pool next to the rock wall and then drops off into a deep sinkhole. I listened to the falling water and noticed that it made a strange echoing sound, so I climbed into the hole. There I found a series of underground passages that led off in different directions."

Kase grinned and nodded, and Asher smiled back at him.

"I didn't have a light with me, so I followed the

only one that wasn't too dark to see the walls. I guess I got lucky, because it opened into the box canyon we're looking for."

Murdox looked at his beaten paws with little enthusiasm. "Hurrah…."

Kase jabbed him in the ribs. "Don't mind the dog. That's great news!"

*

The weary group followed the river and hiked into the ravine until they arrived at the spot Asher had found. Sure enough, it looked as though the river simply fell away into darkness, but Asher pointed them to a series of loose boulders that led down into the hole. Asher then climbed onto the closest boulder and gave Kase and Murdox a helping hand to follow him. The group traversed the boulders and navigated through a series of long, twisting passages.

Eventually the cave gave way to the box canyon they sought. Its sheer walls loomed overhead, obscured only slightly by a few small trees that clung tightly to the rocky face. All they could see of the sky was a thin blue streak far above their heads. It was getting late in the day, and the shadows on the canyon walls grew longer by the moment.

They had marched for about an hour when the canyon suddenly gave way to a breathtaking vista. Here their path ended in a sheer drop-off. In front of them stood the seemingly endless jagged peaks that certainly earned their name and dire reputation: The Dragon's Spine.

Asher pulled out the map and studied it carefully.

"This should be it," he told them. "The entrance to the cave has to be around here somewhere."

Each of them scrutinized the canyon walls as they went along. To both the left and right, the rock walls disappeared far overhead. In front of them was nothing but a drop-off, falling straight down, thousands of feet below.

Then suddenly Murdox came to a stop and looked high above them toward the rock face.

"Shush! Do you hear that?"

Kase looked over at him. "Hear what?"

Asher put his hand to his ear and then said, "Murdox is right. That's the sound of the wind whistling. There must be a cave up there." He then spotted a slight discoloration in the rock wall. "Yes! That's the cave we're looking for!"

Kase peered up the wall with a quizzical look.

"I don't wish to be a party pooper, but a lot of good that does us, way up there. I'm a good climber, but no one could make it up that face."

The three of them felt beaten. It seemed as though they had made it all this way for nothing. Murdox suddenly grabbed for Kase's backpack. He opened the flap, climbed into the bag until only the bottom half of his body could be seen, and rummaged through the contents. Kase and Asher were simply too tired to question the wolf-dog.

Murdox apparently found what he was looking for and withdrew himself from the magical pack. He blew away dust from the cover of an old photo album he had retrieved and quickly flipped through its pages with furry paws.

"I knew I recognized this spot. I just couldn't remember where I'd seen it before. I had known your Aunt Zelda for years before you and your father stumbled into our world." The wolf-dog looked up at the boy. "She was behind the plan of getting you two here, you know."

Murdox studied the boy's eyes for a reaction, but Kase didn't seem very surprised. "Well, anyway, she sure was a wild old girl with a great love for treasure hunting." Murdox pointed to a plump little balding man in the picture. "She and this guy must have been here before."

Kase studied the photograph.

"I don't recognize the guy, but this is definitely my aunt… and this photograph looks exactly like where we're standing."

Asher, who had only been remotely interested in the conversation, suddenly took a better look at the image.

"Wait! Look at this picture closely. Where is that little grate behind them?"

Kase and Murdox saw what Asher was pointing

at, and all of them looked for the exact spot where the picture had been taken. Asher walked over to the canyon wall. Shrubbery had grown high onto the rock face, but after some searching, he pulled aside an overgrown bush and uncovered the well-hidden grate.

Asher rubbed his chin. "Over the years, this shrubbery must have concealed the entrance. Your Aunt Zelda must have known about this place for years."

Using Kase's picking tools, they went to work on the grate. Finally, the ancient lock snapped apart with a click, and the iron grate squeaked as it opened on rusty hinges. Kase pulled a lantern from his pack and held it inside the entrance to the small tunnel. He peered into the darkness.

"You think Aunt Zelda actually went in here?" he asked.

Murdox just shrugged. "I wouldn't doubt it for a moment."

They crawled one after the other into the putrid tunnel. Slime coated the slick walls of the narrow passage before them, and the air reeked of decay. They had to wade on their hands and knees--even Murdox had to creep along on his belly--to reach the end of what they hoped would be a short passage. Their hands squished into soft muck that oozed between their fingers. No one dared look down to see if it was actually mud they were feeling. They simply carried on further into the abyss.

Sweat trickled down their faces, and Murdox panted uncontrollably as the air became increasingly rancid. The tunnel seemed to stretch on for an eternity, and the smell seemed to be getting worse by the second, if that was possible. Gagging from the stench, they nearly turned back; but by the time the air became too noxious to breathe, the passage widened and began rising out of the fetid waters.

With great relief they found that the passage was now large enough to stand, and the air became bearable once more. Asher and Kase rose to their feet, stretched, and tried with little success to wipe the scum from their clothes. The flickering light from their lantern danced off the slimy walls, casting ominous shadows on the smooth green surfaces. They now stood in a vaulted room that seemed to be at the center of many outward-branching tunnels.

A sudden sound in the distance startled them. A rumbling noise seemed to be coming from one of the many surrounding passages and quickly grew louder. Then a column of water erupted from a nearby tunnel and cascaded into a frothing pool of liquid, ever deepening around their feet. Tunnel after tunnel exploded with a rush of incoming water. It was due time to make haste out of there.

With Murdox and Kase following behind him, Asher dashed under a low archway hardly wide enough for their shoulders. They raced down a damp corridor that stretched off into the distance. The sound of the rushing water was nearly deafening. Their feet started to slosh, and they realized that the water had already caught up with them.

The torrent of black water was up to their knees when the corridor finally came to an end. They climbed a narrow ramp and clambered onto a ledge that sat just above the rising water. Then they scuttled to the end of the ledge and ran into a dead end.

A rusted ladder protruded from the rock wall in

front of them, its rungs disappearing into the gloom far above. With the water rising rapidly, it didn't take the group long to decide which way to go. Luckily the ladder was stronger than it had first appeared. With Murdox hastily tied to Asher's back, they climbed carefully upward until their ascent ended at a heavy metal door that resembled a thick flap with hinges at the top.

Kase, who had climbed up the ladder first, exerted all his strength just to nudge the door open a slight crack at the bottom. He called down to Asher. "Can you help me with this?"

Asher scrambled up next to Kase, and they both pushed at the heavy door. Asher bent his head low and put his shoulders into the job. He heaved with all his might, finally moving the door inward enough to enable Kase to squeeze between the door and the floor. By wiggling and wedging himself underneath, he was able to slip through the opening. Then with Asher pushing from below, Kase braced himself with his feet and dragged on the heavy iron door until he managed to throw it open. Asher and Murdox climbed through the opening, emerging in a small cavern.

Asher looked around at the cave walls. "Those passages must have been some kind of old mining tunnels that were connected to the natural cave. I think the dwarves of old must have worked these areas even before the Ancient Wars. I suspect that they abandoned them either when the dragon moved in or when they unwittingly discovered the underground spring that must flood these tunnels periodically."

Murdox shook the water from his fur and further soaked Kase and Asher.

"I suspect the latter." Their voices echoed through the many tunnels. They looked up and down each of the passages, which branched off in several directions. Murdox snuffled and breathed in the cavern air, but it didn't require his canine senses to determine which way to go. They could all smell the malodorous stench of a dragon emanating from a tunnel directly ahead of them. They followed their noses and headed into the deep, dark passage.

Kase held his lantern up to the walls, and it illuminated soot stains that had blackened the ceiling of the tunnel.

"Looks like we're headed in the right direction."

Asher and Murdox looked worried and nodded agreement.

For the better part of an hour, they followed their noses. The tunnels branched off many times, but each time they chose the most odorous path. The air in the tunnel was cool and damp. Gradually the sulfurous stink of the dragon began to be overpowered by a more pungent stench of death and decay.

The tunnel ended abruptly in an alcove that overlooked a vast cavern. The smell of death was overwhelming, but what they saw in the cavern made them forget about the stench entirely.

Bones of every conceivable shape and size littered the cavern floor. They were stacked and thrown in random heaps, all in various stages of rot and decay. What immediately arrested their attention was that as far as the dim light would allow them to see, the entire cavern was awash in gold. Jewels of every imaginable color lay scattered across the floor. Priceless antiquities were intermingled with the rotting bones, strewn about carelessly like nobody's trash. The staggering sight of it all left them speechless.

A moment passed, and then Kase lifted his head.

"Do you hear crying? I could swear I hear sobbing in the distance."

Murdox and Asher hardly heard him. They were still trying to digest the sight of the sea of gold that lay before them.

Suddenly a deep, snarling voice echoed through the cavern.

"I can smell thieves in my house!"

The little company broke out of their trances and ducked back into the tunnel behind them. Kase fished through his pack as they ran several yards down the narrow corridor. Then he dropped his bag to the cavern floor and in a cloud of dust, removed two slightly used full-length firemen's jackets and one shorter one, along with red hard-hats.

"Glad I borrowed these from the fire station downtown. I thought we might need them sometime." Kase handed Asher a long jacket and wrapped the shorter one around Murdox.

Kase and Asher quickly donned the longer fire-resistant coverings, and they all ran a little farther back down the tunnel. A low hissing sound filled the cavern behind them. They turned and looked back to see angry, glowing, yellow eyes staring at them from the rear of the tunnel.

"I can smell you," a guttural voice rumbled.

Smoky, sulfurous breath blew down the narrow passageway toward the three companions, nearly choking them. A blood-red head appeared, smiling and exposing a double row of sharp teeth that extended back into the dragon's mouth for what seemed like miles.

The dragon hissed and then mused, "I didn't order any food delivered, but I think I could manage something roasted...."

The blood dragon reared her sinuous neck and tossed her head. Then she thrust her great neck forward and opened her ghastly mouth. A wave of fire bellowed from her widespread jaws and engulfed the tiny tunnel.

The three travelers dove to the floor to protect themselves from the flames. Only the jackets prevented their being burned alive.

After the fire passed over them, Kase stood up and rubbed his singed eyebrows. "That wasn't as bad as I thought it might be," he reflected.

Asher leaped over to the wolf-dog and stamped on his smoldering tail. Murdox yelped in pain and growled as he tried to brush burning soot from his fur with his paws.

A gray curl of smoke drifted from the dragon's nostrils as she peered with glowing eyes deep into the tunnel.

Kase lifted his head and spoke in a respectful voice.

"Excuse me, madam, but we don't want your gold. We just need your help."

The dragon took a step back. "So, the little thieves speak…. Why aren't you dead?"

Kase scrunched up his nose and defended their honor. "Actually, ma'am, we're not thieves. We're agents for the Incantation Enforcement Agency… well, Murdox and I are. Asher is a ranger for the elf kingdom of Greylok. We really do need your help."

The dragon hesitated for a moment. "…and why

should I help thieves?"

Kase decided to get right to the point. "Like I said, we're not thieves… we simply need an ingredient to save the great King Drake Bremsford of the Elvin Nation of Greylok. He's sort of turning to stone…."

The dragon again reared her head, and the three companions dove to the ground once more. Instead of breathing fire down the tunnel, she began to laugh. She laughed so hard that she finally choked on her own gray-black smoke.

"I guess your king has gotten himself into quite a pickle," she said, and she started to laugh again. After a while, her laughter began to subside, and she began to weep. The great blood dragon with scales of steel and claws like sabers actually began sobbing like a baby.

Kase made his way up a narrow stone ramp to an alcove that overlooked the vast cavern. The dragon threw back her head and blew fire to the ceiling above her. Flames danced across the roof of the cavern, charring the walls black with soot. Molten rock from the engulfed ceiling fell into the gold below, creating gleaming pools of liquid metal on the cavern floor.

Kase then climbed down the rocky ledge that led into the sea of gold and walked right toward the dragon. Tears rained from her yellow eyes as she rolled onto her back, spreading gold in every direction. The dragon rolled back and forth, sobbing uncontrollably. Kase sat down next to her head and waited patiently for her to regain control of herself. Eventually she stopped wailing long enough for Kase to try to calm her down. The dragon sobbed quietly and slowly rolled onto her side, being careful not to crush the young man.

"You're an awfully brave little thief, aren't you?"

Kase was looking directly at her. "What exactly has gotten a big dragon like you all upset?"

The dragon gazed into the boy's eyes. Kase felt a chill run down his spine, but he held her gaze. The dragon must have been satisfied with what she saw, because she relaxed visibly and began to tell her tale.

"Every thousand years or so, a female blood dragon bears an egg... just one egg, mind you. It's a beautiful thing, small and delicate, all shiny black with little red swirls. The egg takes nearly a hundred years to incubate and hatch."

She sniffled and let out a little puff of smoke. "Many years ago I bore just such a precious egg. For safekeeping, I put my baby-to-be in a quiet little warm spot, off in the corner." She pointed an immense claw in the direction she was speaking of. "Well, I guess about eighty or ninety years passed, and I was feeling a wee bit tired. You see, I had just sacked a village on the other side of that sandy ocean, and I think I ate someone who simply didn't agree with me. I've got a bit of a weak stomach, you know, and foreign food sometimes just doesn't settle right.

"Anyway, I thought I'd feel better if I could catch a few winks, so I laid my head down for what I intended to be no more than just a couple of years… but when I woke and checked on my egg… my future baby was gone."

The dragon reared her head and howled in defiance. Her deafening roar shook the cavern walls. Then she went on, "I smelled trolls. Thieves had entered my home in the night and stolen my egg!"

Kase looked over at Murdox, who with Asher's help had quietly climbed down the ledge and was standing next to him. Kase had that familiar gleam in his eye, and Murdox knew what the boy was thinking.

Kase began speaking in a professional-sounding voice. "About how long ago do you think this occurred?"

The dragon counted on her claws. "I don't know. Time is so silly to us dragons. I've been searching for a while now. I guess about three or four years ago, give or take a couple."

Kase worked the math in his head. "Well, I guess that about coincides with what I was thinking."

He and Murdox turned their backs to the dragon and quietly discussed the situation. Asher and the dragon waited patiently until they had finished.

Kase looked back at the dragon and explained, "Just under five years ago, my father and Murdox here were searching some tunnels under the city of Cloudview... Murdox was a man then. Anyway, they ran across a sewer tunnel full of trolls. Well... I'll let Murdox tell the tale...."

Murdox then retold how he and Brent Hobskin had been captured and escaped from the troll encampment. "During our escape, Brent spotted an egg exactly as you've described yours. It just happened to be in the same room where they kept us. We knew it was a dragon's egg but had no idea at the time which variety it was. When we escaped, Brent grabbed the egg... he wasn't about to leave something so valuable with the trolls. I can only imagine what they might have done with it."

The dragon tossed her head in rage and roared at the very thought of filthy trolls handling her egg. Then she leaned down, anxious to hear every word.

Murdox continued, "So, anyway, as we slipped away, Brent grabbed the egg and stashed it in his pack. I didn't know what had happened to it after that."

Kase spoke up. "But I do. When Murdox and my dad returned to the office to round up the Enforcement Squad, my father pulled the egg from the bag and gave it to me for safekeeping. I put it in the evidence locker so that we could figure out which species it was when he got back... only he never did. One thing led to another, and I guess we just completely forgot about it. But I guarantee it's still there, warm and safe. According to my calculations, depending on how long you actually slept, you still have a few years before it hatches."

Murdox put on a big doggy grin and addressed the dragon. "I think we can come to some sort of agreement here."

The dragon was so happy that she flapped her massive wings in glee, blowing the companions to the floor. "If what you say is true, and that really is my egg, I'm sure we can arrange something. Yes, absolutely, we most certainly can!"

The next thing they knew, a splendid deal had been hashed out, and they were nearly on their way. Using assorted supplies from Kase's pack, Asher fabricated a makeshift seat for each of them. The dragon lowered her head to the floor of the cave and allowed each of the companions to climb onto her reptilian back. She waited for them to situate themselves comfortably while she prepared for the journey.

The dragon circled once around her makeshift runway and then moved to the back of the cavern. She dropped her forearms to the ground and with her hind legs, she began to run in place. She whipped up a huge cloud of dust and then let off the brakes.

Then she was hurtling down the runway of the cave. An instant before reaching the edge, she leapt high into the air. The companions were pressed into the backs of their seats as the dragon vaulted toward an opening at the top of the cavern, and the floor dropped out from beneath them. Kase looked for the ground, but thousands of feet separated them from terra firma. Cold damp air rushed past their faces as the dragon unfolded her great, leathery wings and climbed into the sky.

They were borne upward on the wings of the dragon, in high style, soon to complete their mission. The dragon's giant wings beat the air into submission as they climbed high into the sky, soaring effortlessly through the cool air and slicing through the big, puffy, white clouds.

Kase's eyes started to water, so he grabbed a pair of goggles from his bag and slipped them over his eyes. Wind whipped across their faces, and for some unknown reason, Murdox just had to fulfill an overwhelming desire to stick his head out to the side and hang out his big, slobbery tongue. This seemed to give him great pleasure, and neither Kase nor Asher had any desire to pull him back in.

Kase spotted the leonine village below them and asked the dragon to give the creatures a good scare. The dragon made a lazy turn and banked over the village where they had been prisoners just a day earlier. She could easily have blasted away the village with one giant fireball, but the party instead opted for her simply to swoop in low and shake them up a bit.

As they desired, she dove straight for the village and feigned an attack, spreading wide her gaping jaw. The leonine saw her coming and panicked in utter terror. The massive dragon flew in close, barely skimming over the ground and causing everyone in the village to drop to their bellies. Her powerful wings produced a pressure wave strong enough to knock over the few brave souls who dared hold their ground to challenge her.

Murdox yelled at the top of his lungs, "Take that, you overgrown house cats!"

Once the fly-by was completed, the dragon simply pointed her head to the clouds and accelerated effortlessly back into the sky.

From there the dragon flew tirelessly in the direction of the Great Forest, resting only once on their trip back to the castle. Kase decided that winging their way on the back of a dragon was the only way to travel.

Within a day and a half, the forest came into view. The dragon dove in low over the treetops, throwing up a wake of leaves in passing. By the middle of the eighth day of their adventure, Greylok was again in sight.

The blood dragon circled the castle as Kase and Asher yelled to the elves below. She came in low and made a perfect landing on the finely manicured lawn, directly in front of the King's estate.

At first, the sight of a dragon landing on the front lawn of the castle terrified the locals. In an instant the castle guards surrounded the blood-red beast, brandishing gleaming elven weapons in her direction. Asher waved his hands in panic, trying to make them understand that she meant no harm.

Enob rushed to the dragon's side and forced the guards to stand at ease. The wizened old wizard looked up at the little group and smiled. "All we need is a claw," he joked, "not the whole dragon!"

That broke the tension, and Enob signaled the Queen's handmaidens to approach the beast. Three dainty little women ran over to the dragon with gardening tools and meticulously tended to her claws. A carefully trimmed talon was then handed to the wizard, who in his excitement tripped over his purple robes in a rush to get back to the King.

The handmaidens were examining the dragon's other claws. "Tsk, tsk, tsk…," remarked one of them. "You're in a desperate need of a good manicure." All the ladies took a good look at her claws and nodded in agreement. Then they grabbed tiny stools and started gabbing about castle business while they filed and polished her toenails.

Enob was in his laboratory preparing the constituents for the new potion when Kase and Asher caught up with him. He added the final ingredient, brewed up the potion, and mixed it into a glass of iced tea, with tiny green mint leaves decorating the side.

When they arrived in the King's bedroom, everyone there was hovering around the bed with tears in their eyes. Most of the court had given up hope. The King was a terrible sight. His skin was white and almost completely solid to the touch. The poison in his veins had spread and had taken its toll. It was slowly creeping through his body, hardening all his joints and turning him completely to stone.

In desperation, the Queen quickly poured some tea into His Majesty's mouth, and they all waited with baited breath for any sign of a change. At first, nothing happened. Impatiently the Queen poured in more tea as everyone watched anxiously.

Then Kase spotted a faint sparkle in the King's eye. Slowly the stony flesh began to change color. Gradually the King was able to move his fingers and toes. His true color began to return, and his eyes smiled warmly at all who were watching. Kase noticed the golden crest of the House of Bremsford materialize on the King's chest as if actually carved in stone--a great eagle with a sword in one talon and an oak branch in the other. Kase smiled broadly. The King's green eyes shimmered, and he smiled back at the boy.

Just then, completely destroying the touching

moment, the blood dragon tapped on a windowpane and pointed to an imaginary watch on her wrist.

Kase looked at her and held up a finger, then turned back to the King. "Right, we'd best be on our way, Your Majesty. I'm afraid we still have other business to attend to. I'm sure Enob will be more than able to handle any further symptoms you might have, sir. Take care of yourself, and we wish you good health."

Kase withdrew some paperwork from his backpack and handed it to Enob. The wizard read through the documents and signed his name on the bottom line.

Everyone else watched them, trying to figure out what was going on.

Kase and Murdox looked up from their contract. "The job's not done until all the paperwork is signed," Kase reminded them.

The small crowd looked on in amazement, wondering if this kind of thing happened every day.

Enob returned the signed papers to Kase, who reviewed them briefly with Murdox. He and Kase then nodded in agreement and headed toward the door.

A warm hand touched Kase's shoulder. It was the Queen, who then led them back to the royal bed for a final word with the nation's ruler.

The King sat up and smiled again at Kase and Murdox. "I cannot begin to express my immense gratitude. I mean this from the bottom of my now-strongly beating heart. If ever I can do anything for the two of you, please let me know."

They thanked the King for his gracious offer, bade him farewell, and left his side.

Just out of earshot, Murdox snorted. "*Humph!…* wait till he gets the agency's bill."

Kase only smiled.

Asher had been waiting patiently by the door and followed them out of the room so they could say a proper goodbye.

"There's nothing else left to do here. I'll return to the port city with a few of the stable boys and collect the squirrels. Farewell, my friends. I trust we'll meet again under less pressing circumstances."

Kase and Murdox said brief goodbyes and then

departed the castle.

The blood dragon dipped her head impatiently and allowed Kase and Murdox to climb aboard. With a running start, she tore across the perfectly groomed front lawn, scattering grass and dirt in every direction before she leapt into the air.

Again they were sailing over the treetops, headed for the city of Cloudview. Within the hour they left the Great Forest in a wake of swirling leaves and were cruising high above the vast plains. A few smaller dragons and an enormous eagle swooped over to check them out but quickly realized that this was no creature to disturb.

Out of the corner of his eye, Kase spotted a trug tooling across the ground in its high-speed commute to the forest. It seemed like only yesterday that they were riding along inside such a machine, oblivious to what the next few days would hold in store.

When he figured they were within telephone range of the city, Kase attempted a call to the IEA Headquarters. He only managed to get a recording, but left a detailed message. He advised the agency that he and Murdox would be flying through the city on the back of a blood dragon, and it would be nice if they didn't get shot down in the process. He explained the situation and asked that a flight path be cleared. He was hoping for an escort into the congested city and clearance for a rooftop landing at HQ.

The dragon swiftly approached the busy skyways of the city, searching for a place to merge into the traffic. She'd soon had just about enough and was preparing a fireball to blast her way in when Kase spotted a convoy of Dragonflies flying straight toward them.

Kase pointed to the fast-moving aircraft. "This looks like our escort."

Instead, the lead craft fired its particle weapon just over the dragon's head, and a voice was projected over an outside speaker: "You are in restricted airspace. This is a No Dragon Fly Zone. Your presence is prohibited."

In response the dragon suddenly veered to the left.

Murdox commented, "Doesn't look like much of

a welcoming committee."

Kase pulled out his cell phone. "I'm guessing they didn't get my message. I suppose I had better try again."

The lead Dragonfly didn't bother repeating the message and immediately resumed firing on the dragon. This time there was no warning shot, and the dragon had to practice some pretty interesting evasive maneuvers.

Murdox hung on for dear life and yelled, *"Yeah... call someone!"*

The dragon dove headlong into the traffic lanes, narrowly missing an oncoming air taxi. She flew downward, accelerated, and then pulled into a shallow climb. With renewed speed she slipped into the traffic, banked to the left and then to the right, skimming over and under the oncoming vehicles and narrowly avoiding numerous collisions.

The Dragonflies dropped out of formation and took up the chase. They were apparently doing their best to get a clear shot in all the traffic. The dragon barely avoided being barraged and immediately slipped between two glass skyscrapers, quickly drawing her wings in against her sides.

Kase was experiencing a bad case of déjà vu. "Watch out for the flagpole!" he yelled.

The dragon instantly dipped her head, slipping by just inches below the pole. She made another hard dive downward, weaving through the inner city commuter traffic. She continued her rotation and then pointed her body straight down, diving directly for the ground. Kase and Murdox had to hold on for dear life.

A moment before impact, the dragon pulled out of the dive, throwing Kase and Murdox into the backs of their seats. She leveled out a few feet over the ground and headed for the edge of the city. She was forced to swerve between buildings, the tips of her wings skimming the glass and steel walls. She banked low and made a hard turn to the right, lifting her massive body up on its edge.

The two passengers were white-knuckled and screaming at the top of their lungs. Kase yelled over the noise of the city, "At least we're not being carried away to be eaten for lunch!"

Meanwhile, the Dragonflies were still in hot

pursuit. One of them managed to slip in behind the blood dragon and fire a homing missile. The dragon sensed the danger and made a series of evasive maneuvers--up, then down, left, right, and up again--but the missile was still fast on her heels. She came in low, trying to duck under a breezeway between two buildings.

Murdox screamed, *"This is a dead end, I'm sure of it... a dead end!"*

The dragon was already on top of the situation. The passage between the buildings ended abruptly, and another building blocked the way ahead of them. There was no room to turn around, and the missile was closing fast. At the last second, the dragon veered straight upward, pressing the two riders far back into their seats.

They were all screaming, including the dragon. Her belly was skimming the face of the building when she burst over the rooftop. The missile slammed into the side of the building and exploded in a ball of flame far below them. Then the dragon swooped back up into the traffic lanes and tried to lose her pursuers in the congestion. She was weaving in and out of the traffic, popping up and over numerous vehicles that got in her way.

Kase was still trying frantically to reach One Wizard Place on his phone when he finally got a call through. It was the same woman with whom he had spoken the last time he was in a panic during the Gold Trust raid.

"Hold on!" the boy screamed as they ducked in unison, narrowly avoiding a bridge. He tried once again to explain their predicament to the operator. "Please, just contact Commander Crashblade... it's an emergency!"

As the dragon made a sudden spiraling wing-roll in an attempt to avoid yet another stream of oncoming gunfire, the phone fell out of Kase's hand. When she exited the roll, she was flying upside down, allowing Kase and Murdox to watch the phone fall hundreds of stories to the ground below.

Murdox moaned. "That can't be a good thing. Hope you've got a good warranty plan...."

"I think I got through to her. Let's take our chances and head for the office."

Kase relayed the directions to the dragon and

described the building she needed to find. Still flying upside down, the dragon dove out of the traffic lane and swooped over the edge of the city. She peeled off a few hard turns, in and out of a series of power conduits, and narrowly avoided slamming into the side of a water tower.

Fortunately every level of the city was numbered, so she found the right one easily. She was searching for One Wizard Place when a swarm of Dragonflies popped out of nowhere and surrounded her. She attempted to dive lower into the city, but a squadron of the ships blocked her path. When she attempted to climb out and away from them, another influx of aircraft prevented her escape.

Just when they thought they'd bought the farm, the lead Dragonfly turned an about-face and courteously attempted to pace the dragon's forward flight path. One of the airships headed in and made a narrow fly-by. It matched its speed with the graceful dragon and came alongside her, lowering its aft cargo ramp. There, harnessed to the ship, was Commander Crashblade.

He yelled through a bullhorn over the wind

noise, "Sorry about the misunderstanding! How about an escort the rest of the way in?"

Crashblade waved, and the aircraft accelerated past the dragon. It took position just in front of her nose and led the way to the rooftop landing pad of One Wizard Place.

The dragon gracefully glided down in a perfect two-point landing. She roared with excitement, "Whew, what a workout! That was the most fun I've had in years!"

Kase and Murdox were still shaking from nerves as they climbed down from her back. Stammering, Kase told her, "We'll be… be right back."

Murdox was a bit wobbly on his pins, but with each other's help, he and Kase managed to make it into the building. They headed straight for the office without further distractions. Kase unlocked the door and tossed his backpack on the couch. He hurried into the evidence room and spun the combination lock on the metal vault. Murdox stumbled in next to him and helped him open the door.

Kase then switched on the overhead light and

unlocked a yellow cabinet that opened smoothly on well-oiled hinges. They were relieved to see that everything was still in its place.

Kase uncovered the egg and recognized the markings the dragon had described. Then he dug into his backpack and found a soft blanket. He withdrew the egg carefully and wrapped it in the blanket. Then they carried the egg back up to its eagerly waiting mother.

The blood dragon eyed the egg with a glowing yellow stare and then peered at Kase and Murdox. They shook with fear, afraid they might pass out right on the spot if it wasn't the genuine article. Then she lifted her head to the night sky and howled with relief. She sobbed for a few moments and then rolled out a gargantuan, pink, forked tongue, licking them both from head to toe.

They couldn't be happier. Inside a week they had been beaten, battered, and pushed to their limits, and now they were completely covered in dragon slobber.

At this point, the landing pad was awash with curious onlookers. To everyone's great relief--especially Kase's and Murdox's--this was apparently the right egg. The dragon thanked them again and promised she would try to get back for a visit after the baby was born. Then she bade them farewell and clutching her precious egg, flew off again as they tried in vain to wipe the goop from their clothes.

Two very tired agents headed back toward their office to finish their paperwork. Commander Crashblade caught up with them in the hallway and again apologized for the earlier misunderstanding. Apparently no one had gotten the message until the attack was underway, and by that time Kase had already phoned back. The commander handed them his personal phone number so that such unfortunate incidents might not occur in the future.

Crashblade then thanked them again for their help in the Gold Trust raid and told them that the Force was hot on the trail of those who were behind the whole thing. He said he would keep them informed and told them to take care. Just then, his pager went off. They said their goodbyes and parted.

The weary agents then staggered into the office and crashed on the couch. The phone began ringing, but neither of them had the energy to pick it up. They let the machine answer and noticed the subsequent message light.

Murdox rolled over onto his back. "We'll check on it in the morning."

An exhausted Kase just sat bleary-eyed, staring numbly at the blinking red light and wondering what their next adventure might entail....

Don't miss the sequel to:
ONE WIZARD PLACE

SENTINEL

SENTINEL

In the moment that a cloaked figure named Eldin walks into his life, the world that Fox Strongbow has understood is changed forever. Fox has already known that he is different from other children his age, but little did he know that this stranger would teach him how to use his gift to become one of the elite guardians known as a Sentinel.

Sentinel training takes nine years before an apprentice is ready for his final test. Riding on the feathery backs of giant predatory birds, Fox and his mentor Eldin embark on a perilous journey to test the young boy's skills. The trial takes the two riders to a distant island where they encounter dangerous and elusive creatures that push the young apprentice and his mentor to the limits of their abilities.

On their return from the island, the unthinkable happens,

and the two riders are attacked by a ruthless black dragon that forces them down into the Swamp of Doom and Despair to fight a battle for life or death. Eldin is possessed by the dark soul of the black dragon and becomes a creature known as Drago. Through Eldin's memories, Drago learns of the location of a key that unlocks an ancient artifact said to be more powerful than anything else in the world.

Drago will stop at nothing to obtain this artifact and the power it could bestow upon him. Thus he begins a search for an item that was hidden from the world, never intended to be found. Meanwhile, with two wounded birds in tow, Fox fights a hopeless battle to survive the swamp and return to Greylok to report the awful news.

Fox is rescued from the swamp, only to find that he must stop Drago before he can recover the object that was never meant to be found. To do so, Fox, along with an elven wizard named Enob and two agents from the Incantation Enforcement Agency, take on a quest that sends them to the dregs of the vast city of Cloudview, where they encounter awesome foes and nearly insurmountable obstacles.